I0666846

Hello Canada,
Hello Prairies

Hello Canada, Hello Prairies

MICHAEL POMEDLI

RESOURCE *Publications* · Eugene, Oregon

HELLO CANADA, HELLO PRAIRIES

Copyright © 2025 Michael Pomedli. All rights reserved. Except for brief quotations in critical publications or reviews, no part of this book may be reproduced in any manner without prior written permission from the publisher. Write: Permissions, Wipf and Stock Publishers, 199 W. 8th Ave., Suite 3, Eugene, OR 97401.

Resource Publications
An Imprint of Wipf and Stock Publishers
199 W. 8th Ave., Suite 3
Eugene, OR 97401

www.wipfandstock.com

PAPERBACK ISBN: 979-8-3852-5217-6
HARDCOVER ISBN: 979-8-3852-5218-3
EBOOK ISBN: 979-8-3852-5219-0
VERSION NUMBER 05/19/25

To all prairie people

Contents

Introduction

THE PRAIRIES. NOT so drab. Not just a flat, dreary land. Quite interesting in fact. Like dynamite. This book is a way of saying hello to Canada and the Prairies as the Louie-Anne family embrace life's events.

Even getting rid of stones could be exciting. While picking stones off the field by hand was an onerous task, farmer Louie found a noisy and disrupting way of eradicating the larger ones using dynamite. On some fields there were a lot of small stones which could be gathered into a wagon and hauled onto a stone pile. Others, of medium or large size, had to be rolled onto a flat stone boat and carted away. But there were still additional stones which were large and embedded in the ground.

While some farm implements like a cultivator or disker would generally coast over them, some implements got caught and would bend or break. Louie thought of a partial solution to get rid of these pesky, embedded stones. He heard that a farmer, Rudy, in a nearby town, sold dynamite which could take care of these larger rocks. He visited Rudy, purchased some dynamite and received instructions on how to safely use it to blow out stones.

"The sticks are only eight inches long and look kind of cute and harmless and the blasting cap is very small," Rudy stated. "But they are dangerous stuff. The cap alone could take your arm off. Don't let your boy get too near. One should not generate any type of spark lest when handling the sticks it could ignite the dynamite. Use a wooden probe to make a hole in the stick. Put a blasting cap on a fuse, crimp it with a proper tool, cut the fuse to the desired length and insert the cap and fuse into the hole in the stick. Here is a handbook that you can read.

"Dynamite is a useful tool. It is actually a chemical, nitroglycerin, a compound that made Alfred Nobel rich and famous." Rudy stated. "And it can be used by inexperienced persons who make an effort to learn to use it safely.

"Now there are two ways of dealing with a large stone. The first is to just blow its top off. To do this, lay as many sticks as you want on top of the stone; put a liberal amount of mud to cover it and then light the fuse. Have a long fuse so you can get a fair distance from the blast. The dynamite will blow the top off the stone and then you can put ground on top and cultivate it. The second method is to dig a hole beside the stone in question, insert the stick, cap and fuse and when ignited that should lift the stone out of the ground."

Louie was sold on using dynamite. He bought a dozen sticks and a dozen caps, a crimping tool, and several feet of fuse. He was convinced that this was dangerous stuff and so he stored the material in a locked granary.

He practiced lighting the fuse by itself. He tried various lengths to know how long certain lengths would take to burn. Next, he learned how to crimp the fuse into the blasting cap, using the non-sparking alloy tool. To make sure he had done it right, he again lit the fuse and from a distance observed the cap igniting by itself.

Now he was ready to get at the stone. "With a crowbar I punched a hole about 12 inches deep in the soft ground. I placed the prepared dynamite stick in the hole, covered it with dirt, and tamped it lightly. I lit the fuse—I used a 90 second one—and ran. Then a BOOM! The stone was on top of the soil. From information in the handbook, I calculated that for larger rocks I really would need two sticks of dynamite, one on top of the other or spaced about 18 inches apart."

Louie tried both of the methods Rudy suggested with varying degrees of success. Once he blew a stone out of the ground and through a barbed wire fence, dismantling it.

Later, Louie got the idea of using dynamite to remove a dozen or so stumps from the field. He used two sticks of dynamite, on opposite sides of a large stump. With a grub axe and crow bar he dug between the roots. He inserted the dynamite, filled the holes with ground and tamped them. The resulting explosion cut the large tap root at the depth of the charge and threw the stump about 12 feet into the air. He then quite easily hauled the stump parts away.

"Dynamite was the best tool for many jobs," Louie concluded. "In fact, it was great fun."

From his encyclopedia reading, he learned that Alfred Nobel of Sweden was the first to use dynamite successfully. He was a Swedish chemist after whom the Nobel peace prize was named.

It was a rather long distance to the lake and took the cattle a while to find water in the wintertime. Louie remembered that Rudy had suggested, perhaps in jest, that he could use dynamite to make a dugout. So, this spring, Louie took this suggestion seriously and planned to harness the explosive power of dynamite to create a cavity near his backyard and on the path of flowing water. He needed quite a bit of dynamite for this creation and used a long fuse.

"I will blow a hole to kingdom come," he prophesied.

There was an earth-shaking boom, with mud, and debris flying into the air. After the smoke cleared, he ran back and found a deep ditch. Just what was needed for his cattle. But an hour later he got an excruciating headache from breathing the dynamite's fumes.

So, the Prairies provided a mixture of excitement, experimenting and unexpected results.

1

Personalities

PRAIRIE PERSEVERANCE

Prairie people are a persevering lot. True, many farmers abandoned their farms after giving it their best shot. There was hardship, but also survival. Old, abandoned and rotting buildings brought back many memories for David. Leaning and crumbling, they remained relatively upright instead of being torn down. In it, couples had raised children, grew old and died or moved away. These were monuments to many hopes and dreams, dating and loving, disappointments and successes.

David visited one nearby. Vestiges of life remained inside: a McClary stove where wives slaved, a rusting bed frame, scattered newspapers and books, on the floor an old coat. A torn oilcloth on a table where bread was made, vegetables cut and eaten, homework done, where pioneers sat and talked or played cards, a place where inside and outside met.

There were other farm memories of much manual labor especially fixing fence, and picking stones since nature always pushed them up each spring and became a farm's ordained penance. Louie despised the weeds in the fields. He had tried hard to get rid of them by cultivating and then harrowing. But some persisted, wild oats in the moist slough areas, mustard and sow thistles elsewhere. The family picked even the prickly weeds, gathered them in heaps, let them dry and then burned them.

Planting trees to protect the yard and garden. Tending bees, extracting honey. Enduring the dust devils, the whirlwinds, unlike poet's Pauline Johnson: Oh, wind of the East, I wait for you. Blowing in my face.

UNCLE GEORGE

David liked to walk to his grandparents' homestead, a half hour away. There he visited Uncle George who lived upstairs and seldom moved down to the kitchen for he was paralyzed from the waist down, a result of a bout with polio. Although he had body odor and bad breath, both David and sister Theresa were fascinated by so many new things he had and did. When his father asked David to take school notifications to his uncle for duplicating, he bounced and ran the two miles. George wheeled his chair to his typewriter, inserted carbon paper between the forms and rapidly and skillfully clacked out the required duplicated information.

Short for his age, Uncle George could do so many interesting things: from balsa wood, he crafted and assembled a model airplane, fashioned and played a violin, listened to a crystal set he created, collected stamps, repaired watches, put a paper dress on a nude woman forming the handle on a letter opener, and best of all, and unfailingly, gave Theresa and David each a stick of Wrigley's Spearmint gum.

That stick gave them time for a ritual pause. First, there was the gracious thank you, given since their parents had instructed them properly and also to ensure that there would be future gifts. Then the passing of the stick under one's nose to savor its heavenly aroma. The careful unwrapping of the outside paper, exposing the silver one. Saving that and pulling the flat gum out, dividing it in two, putting one-half back into the wrapper and finally inserting the other half into one's mouth. Smiles and delectation at the same time.

During one early harvest, it was Uncle George who woke up early in the morning, peered through his window and spied flames pouring from the nearby barn. The fire devoured the entire building as well as horses that could not be forced outside.

George visited some health clinics in the United States to try and relieve his pain. When he returned to Saskatchewan, he was hospitalized. Uncle Mike, Louie and David went to visit him and take him some chocolate bars and, of course, Wrigley's Spearmint gum.

David looked forward to that final visit to a favorite uncle. In the hospital entrance, however, authorities indicated that the minimum age for visiting patients was 12. Despite David's age of 9, his father told the nurse at the desk that he was small and short for his age and should be admitted for he was actually 12. The nurse did not believe him and made David wait outside. Sadly, he did not see Uncle George again, for he died a few weeks later.

NEIGHBOURS ANNIE AND GEORGE

As children, Theresa and David had both a fascination and a fear for the couple who lived across from their lake. For one, their farm was isolated from the main road, and, two, Annie and George were brother and sister living together. They began to build their log house and reside in it at the same time as Anne and Louie built their own.

At one time, when Louie, the hired man, and neighbour George were mixing cement for a garage foundation, Anne wrote a note to Annie requesting the use of a trowel for smoothing the cement. David dutifully took it the half mile to the neighbour's house, partly out of curiosity about these people. When Annie answered the door, David noted that she had dark-framed granny glasses and a large growth on her forehead. She read the note, got David the trowel and told him that Anne had misspelled the word, trowel. For verification of the correct spelling, she referred to the Eaton's catalogue. While in the house, David noticed that there were chinks in the logs so that he could perceive the sun beams from within.

At an earlier time, Anne and Louie planned to visit relatives for an evening party. They recruited neighbour Annie to babysit Theresa and David. At this party of relatives, where there was much food, violin and squeeze-box playing, conversation quickly involved children. Mom informed her sister, Theresa, that a neighbour was babysitting us, a rare occasion.

She in turn informed Mom that there was a rumor that the babysitter, Annie, was not well balanced and that she liked to entertain the thought of placing children in the oven just like the witch did in Hansel and Gretel. In great haste, Mom in a panic raised her concern with Dad and they immediately headed home. We were not in the oven, much to our parents' relief, but were all right.

Annie was immediately relieved of her babysitting duties. Since it was late, Annie requested that she stay the night and leave the next morning. After Annie had breakfast, she walked home, but as Mom removed the sheets from Annie's bed, she discovered a lot of lice in them. She then took the sheets outside and thrashed them and aired them.

Occasionally pupils had lice in school and easily spread it to others. Teacher Miss Schmidt then sent notes home on how to treat the lice: comb the hair meticulously, saturate the air with coal oil, take a bath, and boil the bed sheets.

JANOS, THE BSER

After Janos, the hired man, came to the pioneer house for his evening meal, he liked to entertain David and Theresa with music from his mouth organ and also with his stories. Some were really wild. David recalled these enchanting ones full of exaggerations:

"During the bitter winter days, when the temperature dipped below 50 degrees, the magpies needed a team of horses to pull them so they could start flying for the day.

"In the summer time, the heat was so great that mosquitoes grew to such enormous sizes that some wives trained them to do house work and answer the telephone."

Janos had prejudices against some races, for he talked about his mild 70-year-old uncle getting jewed down by the Chink grocers in the neighbouring province. And then after he played Hungarian tunes on his mouth organ, he got a little poetic: "While you work, Hitler was a jerk, Mussolini bit his weenie and now it doesn't work."

In general, Janos was mild mannered but sometimes he swore and vented his anger on the immediate and largest object he could imagine. Strangely, he initially took it out on the hip-roof barn, an easy target.

"That goddam CPR," he cursed as he clenched his fist. "I spit at their engines as often as I can. I hit them and my spit fizzles, but does not make a dent in it. I know I am mad at it, but I have good reasons. They charge for shipping grain to the East and really get lots of money for stuff they ship here.

"I took the passenger train one time and I didn't like it; it was late. It is a monster that brings high fallutin people to the West. But I also have to admit that it is a necessary evil," Janos concluded.

HAIRCUTS WITH JANOS

Having immigrated from Hungary later than Grandpa Istvan and Grandma Julia, Janos Grabica was like an uncle to David. For Louie he was just an old Hungarian, for he played the mouth organ, rode a snazzy bicycle, had a slow and circumscribed European mentality and sang a nursery rhyme which David remembered: *Nyomd meg a gombot! Kapsz egy libacombot,* Press the button! You will get a goose leg. It was a merry, nonsensical song.

David learned that Janos left his wife and two daughters in Hungary and seemed bent on making some money here to send to his family. Louie employed him to do hand work on the farm: splitting wood, haying, stooking, picking stones and stumps. For this he was paid, but there was one job he performed regularly without pay and that was giving haircuts to neighbours and to Louie and David.

On the designated day for haircuts, mostly Sunday mornings, Anne prepared soup, bread and jam to take to Janos, seemingly in return for his barbering. The two males motored to his simple home, engaged in Hungarian talk as they shared news from a Hungarian paper printed in Cleveland and his latest correspondence from his relatives in the old country.

David always dreaded getting a haircut, but especially from Janos. He used a hand clipper which sometimes pulled the hair which he did not seem to notice. While it appeared that Louie never felt distress in the process, David never complained either. The most painful part of the job was when Janos combed David's hair frontward and then used the clipper against his forehead to make neat and straight bangs. David shivered and recoiled with each clipping while Janos urged him to remain still. But Janos understood how to cut hair and did it well, except for the pain caused to David.

Janos was very affectionate with David and Theresa. He was a great story teller and the children found his quaint English quite endearing, using lilly for little, traacktor for tractor.

When David was older, Louie asked him to accompany Janos and another hired man, Walter, to use the hayrack and horses to pick up some loose hay. The pace was leisurely and Janos became more open with his real or imagined stories, although cognizant of the younger member of the crew. He noted that he always wore long underwear even in the summer, although then of a thinner quality. One story involved going to Prince Albert and finding some girlfriends and having a good time. He urged Walter to do the same, for these ladies were very friendly and whenever he visited the city, someone was always on the street to call him by his first name.

AN ECCENTRIC GUY

The district had an eccentric guy, Ben. Sometimes he would appear to be really intelligent, a smart ass and short of stature. David and his friends would mosey up to him, thrust out their chests to show that they were at least equal to him, grown up, if not superior. This did not phase Ben for he ignored them.

He did various jobs for farmers such as picking stones and stumps but he said he really wanted to do nothing, to be a bum and that was a hard job in itself. He sometimes tied one on, for he thought that too many people had expectations of what he should be or become.

"It takes an effort to be a bum," Ben stated. "My neighbours have no idea of my vocation but they continue to give me all kinds of advice. It's like bachelors giving advice on how to bring up children; guys who accomplished the least are the quickest to give most advice. It's all too much, for I really only want to eat, drink, sleep and talk; I really enjoy that.

"I made all kinds of wrong moves in my life: I bought some cattle and the price went down; I cultivated some land and the wheat froze and I gave it away to one of my caregivers. I decided to take on a few jobs, not too much; I wanted to answer to no one but myself. I was a eunuch among the girls.

"As long as I don't break the law, who can say I am doing wrong? I realize I should be doing something for my community, so I ran for village council. Many voiced their opinions about what should be done, like fixing the sidewalks, move junk to make the place more appealing, clean up the manure at the hitching posts to tie horses. So, I did some serious electioneering. I injected a lot of humor into my campaign and it was fun. I thought I might get a few votes. One person said he would vote for me so that I got at least a vote or two and wouldn't feel bad. Guess what, I won by a landslide. At a party, celebrating my victory, I brought a bottle of home brew and shared it with the ladies who, I thought, voted for me.

"Ordinarily I drove a bicycle; it was cheap and I didn't mind being slow. In the winter, I mostly walked or hitched a ride. Guys mocked me, saying I was out of touch, so I bought an old car. I fixed it up so that it ran reasonably well. The first time I drove, I went into a clump of trees; I wanted to avoid them, pulling on the steering wheel and shouting Whoa. I did quite a number for I had to chop my vehicle out of the trees. That was the beginning and end of my driving.

"At first, I didn't care about my clothes; they were somewhat tattered and my pants was held up with binder twine. I wore a shapeless old hat, but on Sundays I put on a clean shirt and tie and new overalls. I felt like an important guy."

AUNT JULIA

A *mulier fortis,* a strong woman, was Louie's only surviving sister, Aunt Julia, or Julie, as he called her. On the homestead, she plied not only inside domestic duties but also outside farm chores. She had an older brother, but was frequently in charge of a growing number of younger brothers and they regarded her as of the same gender, today, maybe, a tomboy. She spoke in a loud, high voice and was given to uttering stern commands.

She married an older German patriarchal type, with land and financial resources. In this household, Aunt Julia was mostly in charge of domestic tasks since she had an increasing number of children but she often voiced her opinion about the propriety and efficiency of tasks on the farmstead. In reluctant deference to her husband, although Hungarian, she spoke German with her children. She milked the cows twice a day and thought it silly for a farm kid to consider babies as arriving via a stork or from a cabbage patch; based on helping deliver calves and her own pregnancies, she knew better.

On the farm and later at her retirement house, she prided on having a large and productive garden. After her husband died in a car accident, she retired again to a larger town where her innate energetic and feisty spirit prevailed. Hungarian bachelors wooed her but she would have none of male dominance anymore; instead, she visited and chaperoned her "womens" and had a lot of independent, spunky fun. Now she had a car, her own bank account and again grew a vast array of beautiful flowers. She continued to spin with the family spinning wheel, crotched, developed her basement using her carpentry skills, and baked her unique and tasty poppy bread.

Aunt Julia always spoke her mind. In town, her car-driving was sometimes a bit erratic and once the local police stopped her, interrogated her, and suggested she consider ceasing to drive because of her age. She resisted, pointing out that younger` people were not necessarily an example of careful driving. Again, she prevailed.

TWO GUN COHEN

Louie needed new boxings or casings for the shafts of his one-way tiller. He had a list of certain farm equipment repairs that could be obtained only at the International Harvester dealer in town. David always wanted to accompany him on those trips, but often had to do farm chores instead. This was early Saturday morning and he had already performed his duties and so eagerly drove along with his Dad.

While in the dealer's shop and on the premises, Louie examined new machinery that had been set up—a rugged, 14-foot cultivator and a new drill with attached packers. He could not afford them at this time, but stored images of them in his memory. At this moment, the repairs alone were expensive enough.

It was already noon and both of them were hungry. They had deliberately not brought lunch along so that they had an excuse to go to a restaurant for a meal, topped with maple walnut ice cream for dessert. They chose Dave's Diner, for although it had Chinese fare and was often called the Chink's, its menu also included the basic meat-and-potatoes menu as well.

"I had this farmer meal before and it was very good, at a reasonable price," Louie commented. Sam, the proprietor, greeted them as they entered. He remembered Louie from his previous patronage. They ordered that basic menu and as they were eating, Sam came to talk to them. He knew they were farmers and he thought he had a story they would enjoy.

"I want to tell you a story about Morris Abraham Cohen. He was a thief in the alleyways of London, England. His parents wanted to reform him and shipped him off to Canada for they thought a new life in the western world with its fresh air and open plains would make a law-abiding citizen out of him," Sam began.

Sam had a charming demeanor and he spoke with an enchanting Chinese-Canadian accent, but these two farmers were puzzled why he was telling them this story. It was not about his Chinese ancestors nor about any specific Chinese person.

"Cohen lived all over Canada, holding jobs on both sides of the law, one as a pickpocket and gangster and the other with training as a boxer," Sam continued. "He had guns on both sides of his hips and therefore earned the name, Two Gun Cohen. His other life was as a farm laborer in Whitewood, Saskatchewan, and also as a worker along the Canadian Pacific Railway with many Chinese laborers. He became friends with a great number of them, something not many white people did in those days. He also began to love Chinese food. One day this appetite led him to a Chinese restaurant in Saskatoon. While he was eating there, two robbers at gunpoint stole money from the cashier. Two Gun Cohen rallied to his defense, beat the thieves, threw them out of the restaurant and returned the money.

"The friendship between Cohen and the Chinese changed significantly after that experience. He became a local hero in the Chinese community. Cohen eventually travelled to China and became for a time the personal bodyguard of China's first president, Sun Yat-sen. He fought with the Chinese against the Japanese in the Second World War.

"I really like this guy and thought you also might like this great story. Enjoy your meal," Sam concluded.

ELI

David went to Humboldt with his Dad to get shovels for their cultivator. Mom also came along to supervise the purchase from Bruser's (Where Everybody Goes) of a properly sized suit to celebrate his Confirmation day. While in the store getting right measurements, a farmer, Eli, like many families, was also shopping. He said he was visiting fellow Jews but thought he should also outfit himself with new clothes.

"I'm actually from Edenbridge, close to Melfort, where my parents homesteaded in 1900," Eli readily introduced himself. Dad and Mom quickly realized that they had a lot in common for their parents also came to Canada at the turn of the century.

"My grandparents turned a few heads when they settled in the area for people were flabbergasted that Jews would be interested in farming. It is true that most of my relatives had little experience in farming. Pioneers thought that Jews were more accustomed to using a pen and running city stores than wielding a double-bladed axe. They could hardly believe that we developed blistered hands, wore bibbed, patched overalls, built log houses and barns chinked with clay and coated with whitewash. After some years, my ancestors thought it was harder and more challenging to be a farmer than a store clerk.

"Some immigrants came from England, some from New York and, with their brawn built a simple, wooden synagogue, and borrowed a scroll. We soon had a rabbi, a teacher and a schochet, a person competent to kill cattle and poultry according to Jewish law. We built a library, had a drama society, and edited a newspaper in both Hebrew and English."

"Wow, your ancestors really accomplished a lot," Louie commented. "My parents and Anne's worked hard on their homestead also. Each side had 12 children and they expanded their holdings greatly."

"My Jewish ancestors said that the land was calling them and thought that owning land was a privilege despite hardships. They were supremely adaptable and were glad to be part of the workers who made the Prairies the breadbasket of the world.

"You maybe heard of Aaron Sapiro who spoke to us and sparked us to embark on a crusade to form three prairie wheat pools."

Louie checked his pocket watch and noticed that quite a bit of time had elapsed. "Your ancestors became such great Canadian citizens, but we have to get on with our shopping. Great to have met you and greetings to your family."

Out of earshot of Eli, Anne and Louie remarked on the many accomplishments in Edenbridge. "We certainly could have kept talking for a long time comparing experiences."

The Louie-Anne family had vague news about the holocaust during World War II. Members of the community who largely had a German background and who spoke German at home felt some unease about what was happening in Germany and Europe. Nevertheless, they sang Christmas carols in German. One of the provincial weekly newspapers was forced to stop publishing in German during the War. Although Uncle Mike was of Austro-Hungarian ancestry, he was not prohibited from joining the Canadian armed forces. In his letters from fronts in Sicily, he voiced his animosity at the German attacks. During the War and after, the family did not know of any Jews seeking and finding or not finding asylum in Canada.

Seeking refuge for these victims was well nigh impossible. It was different for those involved in the Hungarian Revolution of 1956. The Anne-Louie family accepted one of the Freedom Fighters, Sandor, as a farm employee. Sandor and David made a pact that Sandor would help David relearn Hungarian while David would teach him English. They did neither. Sandor's English did not progress too well for he spoke Hungarian to both of David's parents.

2

Farm activities

PRIDE IN THE LAND

"GRANDPA AND GRANDMA TOOK great pride in their land and buildings," Louie noted.to David. "The fields weren't just dirt and the trees merely lumber. They were part of themselves for they toiled to cultivate and use them. While there were demanding jobs both in the house and in the yard and farm, they plied them without complaining. Yes, the cows had to be milked twice a day. The sheep, pigs, chickens, ducks and geese had to be fed and watered regularly.

"Granny loved to give instructions on how to milk cows properly: 'Get the milking stool, sit on the side and somewhat under the cow, take hold of her teats, squeeze and pull down. Usually milk one front one and one back one at the same time and then change and milk the other fat ones. And after the milk quits, take your thumb and finger and keep stripping until you don't get milk anymore. If you only milk a cow half way and leave her, in two or three days she'd be dry. She also quits producing milk if you don't do it regularly.

"'I sang old fashioned songs while milking, especially when I and the cows were content,' your Granny remembered. 'I had to contend with flies buzzing around. If a cow was angry or you pulled too hard and irritated her, she might give a kick, get her foot in the pail or push you into the manure. Cats used to line up since they were always on hand for milking because we fed them. I squirted milk right into their mouths, and always had a cat pan into which I put some fresh milk.

"'I liked raising baby chicks. At first, we had an incubator into which we put eggs. I turned them every other day until they hatched. I usually had a little stove nearby to keep the chicks warm. After they grew bigger, I put them into a larger area. Grandpa kept the chicken house clean. The little roosters got into the frying pan quite quickly while the hens I kept for laying eggs.'"

Summer was a time of family fun and hard work on the farm. Sunrise came early, and everyone got up with the chickens, as they said, to do chores. Plowing the fields and planting crops took place in late April and early May. In August and September, crews of men and horses traveled from farm to farm with a big machine that threshed wheat and oats. Neighbours gathered to help and cooked huge meals for the hungry field workers.

In August, farm women canned and preserved vegetables from the garden. In the fall, the family church arranged an evening meal, preceded by a softball and gambling games. In the winter Louie hunted rabbits to eat at table and to feed the chickens. This was all part of holding down the fort.

TRACTORS NOT HORSES

The family had respect for horses, for although they were generally replaced by tractors, they were still a necessity. Farmers realized that if they wanted them to work efficiently, they had to feed and water them well, curly comb their coats, trim their tails and manes and not overdrive them.

The family had two main horses, a team, Dick and Prince, that performed many tasks: truck grain to the elevator, drive wagons and sleighs to fetch cord wood, and manure the barns; pull a mower and rake during haying season, a rack to haul bundles during harvest and, in winter, direct the family caboose and, with a single horse, a small caboose and cart for school purposes. The family had to treat them well: give them good hay, oats and water; not overtax them for they could give out.

A mild affection for horses; they were good company. Some children wrapped their arms around horses' necks and cried into their manes. Horses appreciated this mood and often turned their necks and craned them to have a better look at these appreciative beings.

While family members stroked and patted their horses, they were not overly affectionate with them. In fact, David liked to caress the nose of his school horse, Lady, then pull on it and tap it vigorously. She became annoyed and bit him in the arm, not really hurting him because he wore a thick parka, but she scared him and he ceased his teasing.

Lady became quite programmed about the duration of her work. On one occasion, as David and Theresa returned from school, Anne told them to take lunch to the field workers. Lady was reluctant to turn around and do some extra work; she resisted at first but then complied. In the field, she was vexed, turned around abruptly and drove the cart's shaft into the fender of Louie' new truck. No appreciation here.

On another occasion, again after school, David decided to get the cows by riding his horse instead of walking. He jumped on Lady and rode a distance bareback. Lady had enough of this additional work; she bucked him off and he fell amid a pile of stones. Unhurt, David tried again but was pushed off Lady's back as she entered a clump of trees with low branches. She was not putting in overtime without protest!

During the long winter evenings, Louie began to share some personal farm history with his son. "Before farmers had tractors, there were limits to farming. Farming with horses meant that you could only work until the horses got tired, two or three hours with the cultivator, challenging for the horses especially when the soil was hard or infested with rocks like large raisins in a pudding.

"Life was geared to the speed and endurance of animals. Horses needed a lot of tending and a few acres of grass land had to be set aside simply to grow the food for each animal. So, there was a practical limit to the size of a cultivated farm.

"With a tractor, however, a farmer could do many more times as much work in the same number of hours, for tractors allowed him to farm up to five times as many acres as he or she could with horses," Louie noted. "An advertisement claimed that one Case tractor replaced 12 horses. A tractor used for work didn't need oats and hay. Land that had been reserved for supporting horses could now be plowed under for cash crops to help pay for the loan it took to buy a tractor."

Tractors could be operated day and night, with little daily care, and were not much affected by hot or cold, insects or pests. Also, gasoline tractors started up instantly, which was a lot faster than having to heat up a boiler to power the older steam ones.

"Yet, tractors were expensive," Louie judged. "To afford a tractor, a farmer had to produce much more which meant farming more acres. These greater investments of money and advances in machinery meant that farmers were forced to get bigger or get out. During the Depression, many farmers gave up on farming, sold out to their neighbours who were only slightly better off. So, fewer farmers with more land.

"Some farmers still thought that the old ways were better, so our neighbour, Bill, built a huge barn for his 12 horses. He needed them in rotation to pull the cultivator, harrows and drill. But really the writing was on the wall. You had to modernize.

"When my parents came to Canada from Hungary, they used the same farming methods that they used in the old country. They cleared the land of trees, ploughed the ground, picked the stumps, smoothed it off with a log or harrows, and used a cultivator type of machine. The seeding process was like nature. Plants release their seeds to the wind or spread them with the help of animals and insects. Millions of seeds are scattered so that a few will find fertile soil to germinate and take root.

"Your Grandpa used a similar method at first by taking a sackful of grain and, fastening it around his neck, he dipped his hand into the seed bag and scattered the grain across his field. But there was an advance to this method. In Rosthern, he purchased a scattering machine, a cyclone seeder; it had a hopper for the grain which he fastened around his neck. Grain flowed down a shaft and over a scattering rotating plate. He turned the shaft with a crank. As he walked up and down a field, he could control the amount and evenness of the spread. A much better way of sowing than by hand. With oxen he then used a log or harrows to cover the grain and ensure proper germination.

"But gradually, farmers noticed that seeds grew better if they found their way slightly below ground where they were protected and would find moisture. Grandpa then purchased a drill which planted seeds in rows and at a proper depth. Since the sown seeds were now at a proper distance from each other, they were not competing for moisture and nutrients. This grain drill, which had a box to hold the grain and deliver the seeds to several discs or hoes, opened up a shallow furrow for the seeds and then covered them. These seeds grew in a uniform manner. At first horses pulled these drills but then tractors took over."

Most farmers could see the writing on the wall that horses were not the way to perform much of the farm work, especially the hard tasks like ploughing and cultivating the land. Although the family continued to keep a few horses, Louie, with his mechanical training in Chicago, looked to tractors as the only way to go.

While he worked with a Rumely-OilPull and a Lanz Bulldog on the family farm, he now bought a used International Harvester McCormick-Deering 22–36 tractor, 22 drawbar horsepower for pulling and 36 on the pulley. It was advertised as "the farmer-engineered powerhouse," making the new farm operation a profitable one and it purported to make the transition from horse power to tractor power complete.

This tractor was billed as convenient to operate: controls with finger-tip response, a roomy driver's compartment, with protection from dust and dirt, ready visibility of both the tractor and the operated machine, compact yet powerful. The seat and seat spring were adjustable for the operator's convenience. Advantages galore: made in the Milwaukee Works factory, it was easy to steer and equipped with 34 ball and roller bearings and had a long life.

"I feel like a horseless farmer," Barney observed. "I don't stop work when I am tired, but I stop when I am done. In fact, during spring seeding I sometimes don't shut off the tractor at night. I read in the paper that the tractor saves a farmer 66 days of labor in a year."

"It is a rarity to see these tractors on rubber tires," Louie noted. "The open-style spade lugs have the nasty habit of packing dirt inside the lug and then churning it around the tractor and into my face. Also, the front steel wheels skid and are almost impossible to turn in soft ground. But this tractor is certainly an improvement over horses."

After having saved money during their work in Toronto, Anne and Louie decided to update their tractors. Immediately on their return, they purchased a new John Deere AR, with R standing for regular or standard front axle over against other versions, including orchard and row crop ones. Louie was influenced by the cute John Deere slogan, Money can't buy happiness, but it can buy a tractor, which is much the same thing!

Although rubber was in short supply during the War, the local tractor dealer assured Louie that the new tractor would have rubber tires. But no, it came on steel wheels. He immediately searched for rims and tires to fit the implement with his desired treads.

Louie read that the John Deere company went back to 1837 when a blacksmith by the same name achieved great success by building and selling a highly polished steel plow. He was a general repairman in Vermont as well as a manufacturer of tools such as pitchforks and shovels. Before the steel plow, most farmers used iron or wooden plows but the soil stuck to them and they had to be cleaned frequently.

The company got into tractor manufacturing in 1918 with its distinctive shade of bright olive-green paint. This colour became part of the equipment's identity, for people could easily tell what kind of equipment was being used. If it was in green, it was a John Deere and there wasn't any question about its worth.

This new tractor had magneto electricity, no lights or an electric starter; operators used a hand cranking flywheel. The clutch lever, throttle, fuel and radiator shutter control were easily reached from its steel seat. It had a comfortable platform for standing, four speeds with a top of six miles per hour. It could pull a six-foot discer or a 10-foot cultivator.

While Louie took pride in his tractor, he was not a fanatic about it and entertained the possibility of purchasing other makes when he had the means. Many owners embraced the motto, Nothing Runs Like a Deere, with a tribal loyalty. They liked the green colour because it reminded them of nature and agriculture.

Hired hand Janos never understood or adapted completely to life on this modern Saskatchewan farm. One clear illustration of this was an incident in late fall when there was a light frost in the air with its gradual and relentless penetration into the soil. To prevent the head of his much-prized John Deere from freezing, Louie drained the water from the radiator each evening.

While Louie was in town, a car traveller slid off a nearby road and walked to the Louie home for help. Janos was sharpening knives on the foot-driven emery stone when the traveller arrived. To extricate the vehicle from the ditch, Janos started the new tractor without putting in water, drove to the site and proceeded to pull the vehicle.

Louie arrived at this moment and asked Janos whether he had put water in the cooling system of the tractor. Although Janos indicated that it took only a short time to do the rescue work, Louie stopped the tractor immediately. In his mind, Janos did not understand that the tractor needed the coolant at all times and that a failure to provide it could result in a cracked block. Luckily, nothing serious happened to that valuable new tractor.

The John Deere dealer gave free of charge to those buying its products a subscription to its magazine, *The Furrow*. The magazine provided its readers with a mix of current issues on farming on both local and international fronts, on best farm practices, as well as exclusive news and facts on John Deere products. *The Furrow* focused on educating farmers about the latest advancements in the field and also shared solutions to contemporary problems. With its enjoyable stories, it looked like a *Farmer's Almanac.*

The magazine also contained several John Deere ads, cooking recipes, and humour. On one cover was a scene of a barefooted boy casting a fishing line into a lake and another, also barefooted, sitting on a fence, with hoe and straw hat in hand, looking down pensively. An endearing poster with tall letters in John Deere green read, Billy loves Charlene. A comment within the magazine was that what really mattered was that the lettering looked good to Charlene in John Deere green.

Louie much appreciated a useful free copy of The Handy Farm Account Book. On the cover was a scene of a farmyard and the notice that the book was issued by John Deere of Moline, Illinois.

David awaited each monthly issue of *The Furrow,* especially the jokes it contained. He remembered a few: The John Deere's manure spreader is the only equipment the company won't stand behind. And another: What do farmers get when their wives run off with the tractor salesman? A John Deere letter!

Another tractor that the family purchased was a Ford 9N with its Ferguson three-point hydraulic hitch. Designed for small farms, it had wide-spaced front wheels and an exhaust routed underneath as in a car. Onto this nifty tractor, an operator could attach a cultivator or bucket and maneuver easily to cultivate gardens or fields, pile stumps or haul manure. Louie never considered colours as important, but some farmers disdained the Ford-Ferguson's dark grey and likened it to sparrow poop. Some thought that John Deere had suggested this terrible colour in order to prevent competition with itself.

Grandpa wanted his large garden in town cultivated so Louie commissioned David to use the maneuverable Ferguson with its cultivator onto this plot. It was a four-mile drive from the farm, but David was happy to oblige. As he arrived, Grandpa was already outside, about to seed his garden. He was in great admiration as David wielded the tractor into the smallest corners and dug up the soil.

As Grandpa approached, David stopped the machine and listened to his broken English. He recalled that some years earlier, he asked one of his 11 sons to disk a few acres nearby with horses. This son whipped the horses to make them step up but he stumbled and fell in doing so. The horses with disc turned around and ran over his leg. "I heard cry and run over and lift disc up. He not hurt too much."

Another job for David: use the Ferguson and its cultivator to gather stumps into windrows and then bunch them into piles. He liked to maneuver this machine rather than use a pitch fork to put the stumps into heaps. He received a nominal sum for his efforts.

BUILDING PRACTICAL KITCHEN CABINETS

Anne and Louie were typical farmers in the Saskatchewan prairie area. Forward-looking, industrious and sure-footed. They showed these characteristics in many endeavors but Louie demonstrated this especially in building kitchen cabinets. In their 1936 home, dishes, pots and pans and flour and sugar were scattered in various open places. To remedy this, Louie kept his eyes open in his experiences of many kitchens while working in Toronto and on the Prairies.

He surveyed the north wall and window of their home and began sketching a plan for a kitchen cabinet development. He had never built such cabinets. Organization was pre-eminent in his mind. A place for all those dishes, pots and pans, but also ample and convenient containers for sugar and flour.

After he completed a rough plan, he purchased plyboard, hinges, pulls, nails and screws for the job. During the fall and winter, he set up his table saw in his nearby shop and he was set to go. He was careful to measure twice and cut once. There were many treks from house to shop.

First, the floor layout, then the frames, the grooves into the various sized doors. He had an idea of how to make the much-used flour available using a v-shaped bin pivoted on hinges and, on a smaller scale, one for sugar also. There was the bright-eyed dumbwaiter, a vertical device to lower and elevate food into the cooler basement, a convenience that won the attention and admiration of his wife and fellow farmers.

All of the lumber had to be neatly sanded and painted, first with a primer and then with white. It was an admirable and useful achievement.

What was farm life like in the late 1930s and into the 1950s? David dreamed about such times and let his imagination loose. Sometimes he was in a half reverie when the present and the past melded.

With his sister Theresa, they lived at Grandma and Grandpas while his Dad and Mom took the train to Toronto to pursue jobs. On their original homestead, these pioneer grandparents fused their past life in Hungary with the Canadian Prairie. Life in Saskatchewan was always new even after living on the same farmstead for 40 years. The vast and open Prairie beckoned them to wonder and explore. They felt privileged to be able to see changes—a result of their backbreaking efforts. There was always something to be done whether in the house or outside, no time for boredom. Always something empty, something to be filled.

While they were somewhat satisfied with their accomplishments, they had no time for complacency, no time for self-congratulation. They embodied the sentiment of their hired hand, Janos, who wisely said that he liked to leave a meal with his stomach not quite filled up. Such a disposition left some space which could be filled. There were always new opportunities.

Prairie dispositions were like that of reacting to a garter snake. The initial feeling is that of fear and revulsion with the drive to kill it. But these creatures quickly slither away. David realized that he couldn't nor should kill such creatures. Not everything should be eradicated nor domesticated. It was like his attitude toward birds—these creatures appear free of charge, out of the blue sky, and provide their colourful presence, and silence and songs. They are joyful and fulfilling, unless they are sparrows or magpies.

WISE FARM REMEDIES

The family's ever vigilant and useful dog leaped through their barbwire fence. She ripped her body from the shoulder to the rear thigh. Louie had heard that a veterinarian could provide aid, but he was too far away and too expensive. David held the squealing animal, while Louie got a large needle and coarse thread and proceeded to stitch her up. Afterwards, Louie nestled her in the dog house, made sure she had lots of food and water and checked on her periodically. She came through the ordeal okay.

In another incident, while driving to school with the cart, David pulled the reins very tight, and the horse drew back in the shafts and her butt grazed the front of the cart only to be lacerated with a protruding bolt. It cut a neat stretch in her rump which started bleeding. As soon as David could, he showed this cut to his Dad who got some calomine lotion and spread it on the affected area and instructed David to do so twice a day. The area healed in due course.

BREAD BASKETS FOR THE WORLD

Many farmers felt that the elevators cheated them. They got short weight, although they received a cheque for their grain immediately.

In the process of grain hauling, David helped his father load 150 bushels of wheat into their Studebaker truck box. They used a portable, external augur carried on the truck box to move grain from the granary. The augur was heavy and it took some time to connect the power take off from the truck to the augur. This was, however, a modern method, for Louie had scooped grain by hand many times in the past, a slow and arduous job.

Now they drove the four miles to the Pool elevator, unmistakable with its label, Use Pool Co-op Flour. Its doors were open and Louie slowly eased the truck up the ramp and onto the elevator's weighing and unloading platform with a receiving hopper beneath.

His permit book had indicated that there was room for a few hundred bushels more on his quota. Such a permit limited the number of bushels that could be delivered based on the extent of the farming operation.

Wenzel, the elevator agent, was there to greet them even though it was Saturday. He and Louie had a business-like but still a friendly relationship.

Wenzel weighed the load and then Louie opened the end gate to let out the initial amount of grain passing through a grate in the floor while Wenzel pressed a lever which elevated the front end of the truck. Meanwhile he took samples of the grain from various places in the box. After both of them had shoveled the remaining grain from the box's corners, he weighed the truck again, this time without the grain and then subtracted this weight to give the correct reading for the grain itself.

David wanted to remain in the cab of the truck in order to experience the delight of being elevated and then peering down on the inside of the elevator. But Wenzel would not permit such a ride for it was rather dangerous and also it might be more difficult to calculate the shift in weight.

In their day, these grain elevators were sentinels on the Prairies, watching over the grain fields and its inhabitants. They were visible landmarks, tall dignified and important, indicating by their numbers the relative importance of each town. This Pool elevator, nestled in front of two United Grain Growers (UGG) ones, was close to 80 feet in height, and leaned a little tiredly beside the railroad track because tons of grain housed for brief periods of time sometimes settled unevenly in elevated bins. An adjacent large annex increased its storage capacity. Inside, bare wooden walls carried the smell of ripe grain, like fresh baked bread, farmers generally agreed.

"It smells a bit like pee to me," David whispered.

Perhaps David was mixing this odor with whiffs of pigeon and barn swallow droppings. He heard birds cooing and wings swishing, for they had many kernels to eat outside and inside. Wenzel, however, tried to keep them out of the elevator itself.

The wooden planks that formed the ramp to the elevator had weathered into a smooth, sculpted hollow. The building groaned and creaked, protesting gusts of prairie summer winds. Inside, near the weigh scale and amid the shadows, were a few shovels, a brush, and some mini posters pinned to the wooden wall; these were gentle reminders to Wenzel of how a lazy elevator operator could cause the structure to lean if he did not keep the levels in the grain bins balanced.

Building an elevator was a momentous event in the life of a community. The structure gathered together the general store and other stores, the post office, the blacksmith and machinery outlets, a school and church or churches. It determined where a town would be located.

Elevators have practical equipment such as vertical conveyor belts, lined with cups or buckets for scooping up grain; these raise loose grain to the top of the building and, from there distribute it by gravity downward into types and grades of storage bins or rail cars.

What fascinated David was the little building connected to the elevator but removed by a stairwell. It was separated in order to get the sparks and heat away from the main building. In this drive shed was a little office where Wenzel did his paperwork and tested grain in the moisture meter. He sold many farm supplies such as fertilizer, herbicides, animal feed, bulk salt, seed, coal, oil, grease, binder twine, lumber, and hail insurance.

A motor room lured David's attention. He peeked through the door but was not allowed to take the stairs to see it up close. He watched intently as Wenzel opened a valve to start this Ruston Hornsby diesel engine. It needed Wenzel's effort to push the large flywheel with his hands and insert a foot into a spoke.

"I have to wind this flywheel up," Wenzel shouted.

David had fond memories of listening to its gentle and rhythmical putt putt as it ran the elevator belts.

"This engine sounds magical and runs like a Swiss watch," Wenzel said as the engine started to puff nervously. "Just wait a little for as it runs its sound and motion will be as smooth as silk."

Wenzel took samples of the delivered grain in order to test its moisture content, to assess its grade, weigh it, and check for any foreign material such as weeds, stones and ground. He then gave Louie a receipt, called a weight or scale ticket, for the number of bushels brought to the elevator. Louie could immediately sell the grain or pay a storage fee and hold the grain until he chose to sell it. He could also get the grain cleaned.

A prominent sign in the elevator was titled Poison Warning. From the Department of Trade and Commerce, Board of Grain Commissioners for Canada, it indicated that there would be a maximum fine of $1,000 for delivering mercury treated grain.

While Louie knew something about the history of treating grain and did it himself every spring, Wenzel thought David should know why the prohibition sign was posted.

"The history of seed treatment goes back many years," Wenzel stated. "Before that time, grain was not treated and the crops suffered from various diseases. Long ago, a ship carrying wheat sank in the ocean and close to shore. Nearby farmers retrieved some of the grain but since it was soaked in salt water it could not be used for processing into flour. However, some farmers planted it. The new crops were free from the diseases of smut and bunt. Bunt is the formation of balls on the heads of grain, or in the case of smut, of blackened heads of infected plants.

"When you crush these balls, you find black powder, smelling sometimes like rotting fish that poisons healthy seeds. So, you can see why farmers began to treat grain with chemical compounds before seeding it. One treatment they use is mercury. It is poisonous, so farmers use face masks when coating grain with it; it also kills birds and other animals that eat the grain that blows off trucks or is spilled on the ground. Humans can also be poisoned from eating the meat from animals that consumed the treated grain."

Since no farmer was waiting to unload his grain, Wenzel concluded. "There are different ways of treating the grain, but a simple one, which your father uses, is to pile the seed to be treated on a solid surface, on a granary floor, for instance, and then dust the top of the pile with the fungicide. Then hand-mix it using a shovel until the grain is evenly coated. Best to use a mask."

David noticed another sign, one that forbade anyone to light a cigarette or smoke in the elevator. The risk of fire from explosive grain dust was very great.

Pointing to the sign, Wenzel said: "I keep dust to a minimum. In today's heat and with this dry air, I try to keep the air flowing. So, you notice that I open doors on both sides so you can feel a nice breeze. I certainly don't want to have an explosion. One time, and only once, when the dust buildup was really great, I had to send a truck home because of the danger.

"There was an explosion and a large fireball in an elevator in a neighbouring village," Wenzel recalled. "Everybody in town heard a loud boom and watched the flames and blankets of thick smoke and clouds of dust pour over the elevator and annex.

"Moving as fast as a galloping horse, the fire spread to the office and engine room. Everyone in the town was rattled. Confusion filled the air. The small voluntary fire department brought barrels of water very quickly but could not extinguish the flames; the whole elevator was consumed and the fire fighters continued to watch the grain smolder for a long time for there were lingering hot spots.

"I drove over there as soon as I heard about it. The force of the explosion blew out several doors and I saw remnants of a few windows dangling along the walls. Fortunately, no one was in the elevator at the time of the mishap."

A truck then pulled up to the elevator and Wenzel gave it his attention.

Visiting the elevator was Norman, a teacher in town. He said he was writing a history of elevators in Saskatchewan and was going to share this information with his pupils.

"Is the present company interested?" he inquired. Louie and David said they were, while Wenzel continued with his paperwork.

"As you know, grain farming is the backbone of the prairie economy," Norman started. "Many homesteaders began by hauling grain to faraway Rosthern at first and then to Bruno and now here. These tall, wooden country structures are necessary for agriculture and trade, especially to eastern Canadian markets and overseas," Norman read from his sketch pad.

"These grain buildings are the creative basket not only of Canada, but of the world. They point in many directions at once: to the farmers who produce the grain, to the town which with its elevators, houses the grain, to the Canadian people who eat the grain and to the world which needs it. Do you know that in 1935 the number of country elevators reached its peak of 5,758, with a capacity of 189.9 million bushels?" Norman emphasized.

Since he had a captive audience, Norman continued. "I fell in love with these towers of silence as I drove from one community to another. So, I read more about them in books and in *The Western Producer,* and the *Winnipeg Free Press.* The silence that I mentioned occurs only from a distance and when it is not in operation. When it is, then it is extremely noisy and dusty.

"I realized that these are really monuments to prairie life; they are their lifeblood. It is prairie people who give them breath and meaning, for they built them, now run them, and rely on them. In many ways, they live in them and sometimes die in them. William Van Horne, who helped build the Canadian Pacific Railway (CPR), developed a policy of encouraging the construction of country elevators at regular intervals, every seven to ten miles along the CPR tracks. This distance was considered manageable for pulling horse-drawn wagons full of grain.

"One of my friends referred to these elevators as pimples on the Prairies in these small, one-horse towns. But as I read more about them, I came to the conclusion that they are more pleasing than pimples; they are like Egyptian pyramids or European cathedrals. They are places where holy things happen such as people gathering together, telling stories, and sharing their food.

"They have become symbols of a prairie way of life, something like the Parthenon in Greece or the Eiffel Tower in France. In fact, artists and architects have made some comments about these structures. Some think they are ugly and unimaginative. Others, like the French architect, Le Corbusier, see them as very handsome for they use primary forms such as the cube and rectangle, straightforward geometric shapes that are clean and sleek.

"They play with the immensity of the prairie sky and endless distances. I think of them as castles in the new world, because they are fortresses of peace, storehouses of plenty and essential links in a chain of trade and commerce. Even though some people consider them as spare and without any fat, they are rich, for where we had teepees and sod shacks before, now we have these unique symbols.

"The Canadian 20-cent stamp gives them prominence, for on it is an illustration of grain harvesting with three prairie elevators in the background. And an elevator appears on the back of a one-dollar bill, giving it widespread circulation."

Even as he continued reading from his notes, Norman still had an audience and so he shared a personal experience: "Sometimes in the fall and winter I stay rather late after school, preparing my lessons and correcting homework. As I walk home, especially when it is snowing a lot or when it is dark outside, I can make out the form of these elevators and then I can figure out how to get home. They are similar to a candle in a homesteader's window at night, a beacon showing a traveller where food, shelter and services can be found.

"I am told that they have guided air pilots who found where they were by reading the names on the elevators. Drunkards used them to reorient their sense of direction and lovers parked their Model T's there and drank beer. It is a sign from God giving me directions. If they are ever torn down, heaven forbid, I would walk like a blind person. When driving on the main road, I would not recognize each town as I went by.

"As a young kid, I remember going by the elevator, dropped in, found some grain, put it in my mouth, and chewed it, a good and cheap substitute for gum for it formed a glutinous, sweet-tasting mess. My parents prized these structures and they bought salt and pepper shakers in the form of elevators.

"I like their red paint, a rusty shade that covers both the Pool and UGG elevators. With their emblazoned company names, they shout the name of each town or village.

"Such was not the case in the early days. Our village was originally five miles from here. It was situated near a trading post for two main trails intersected, or in other places where two rivers joined. In our time, it was the railroads that created settlements so that farmers could haul grain to these tall buildings.

"But the CPR did not own land in the original area and so it ran its line next to their holding, namely right here. It really killed our old town. It could have bent the line, but it didn't and so there was nothing to do but relocate the original town. The stately church still remains on the old site."

When Louie and David were ready to drive home from the Pool elevator, they noticed a small vehicle on the railroad tracks. Wenzel called it a jigger, a small four-wheel railroad car, propelled by a small gas engine.

"It was powered by hand some years ago," Wenzel stated. "To move the car, passengers pushed up and down on an arm pivoted on a base. Mostly section men, those who maintain six to 10 miles of railway track, ride these jiggers. They have to move not only themselves but supplies such as railroad ties and spikes, track nuts and bolts, and shovels—a lot of weight.

"The motor drive now saves a lot of energy and time for the two to four passengers. I saw one that was totally enclosed, protecting the crew. They travel quite slowly, at a maximum of 30 miles an hour and know the schedule of trains so that when one approaches, they can remove the jigger and allow it to pass.

"My Dad worked for the railroad and I and my brother had rides on his jigger when I was young," Wenzel continued. "We'd start walking up the tracks after school so we could catch the section man; he'd always pick us up and give us a ride to the station. I even earned some extra money working for them. After supper, somewhere around six o'clock, if it was snowing, my dad would take me and my brother out to clean the rail switches. We'd get paid for that work."

CREATIVE STEAM WHISTLES

David did not fill the wood box nor did he bring enough water for the stove's reservoir. He was just stubborn and did not want to do his assigned jobs. Anne thought the only remedy she had was to use the old strap. Seeing her brandishing this recourse, he fled to the main bedroom and rolled himself under the twin bed. He thought he was safe from a strapping and seized the springs underneath to propel himself away from danger.

Unfortunately, the springs had sharp edges and cut a slice into the palm and small finger of his right hand. The sight of free-flowing blood and his little finger dangling helplessly alarmed him and made him exit his refuge. Anne was also frightened by the sight, dropped the strap and called into the yard for Louie. He came immediately from the winter cold and applied compresses and helped Anne bandage the wound.

They knew that they needed medical help to stitch the wound and the nearest clinic was 25 miles away. They could not drive that distance with horse and caboose but realized that a passenger train was coming around midnight. Their plan was that the hired hand would drive both Louie and David to catch the train, get the proper stitching done in town and return the next night. The hired hand would then go to town that evening, wait for the train's arrival and return them to the farm.

David recalled seeing the distant train engine that night, spouting puffs of smoke into the clear, crisp winter air. It chugged into the station, steam hissing from its sides, air brakes squealing. The pair went on board and shortly the train took off again and whistled for the next crossing. After he purchased the tickets from the conductor, Louie noticed that he was unoccupied so he began to engage in a conversation, demonstrated his keen interest in things mechanical and asked him about the train's whistle.

"It is called whistling off which means that the train is getting underway," conductor Clarence answered readily.

"A train needs a whistle because locomotives move on fixed rails and are subject to collisions with objects on its path. Such a hazard is increased because the train's enormous weight makes it difficult to stop quickly. So, the train's engineer can warn others of the train's approach from a distance.

"This whistle is inexpensive and is loud and distinct. It is actually a simple device consisting of a bell, the steam opening and a valve. When the lever is pulled, the valve opens and lets steam escape through the opening creating a sound. The pitch or tone depends on the length of the bell.

"Steam whistles are used in factories as a signal for many purposes including the start or end of a shift. Steam ships and light houses also use them. Englishman George Stephenson patented it for use with early trains, actually based on a trumpet, a musical instrument. He thought it was necessary to have them after a train accident when a train hid a herd of cows on a level crossing. Steam whistles soon replaced the trumpets.

"Steam whistles retain their musical heritage in the calliope. This instrument produces sound by sending compressed air, originally steam, through large whistles. A calliope is very loud and can be heard for miles. It has little variation except for its pitch, rhythm and length of the notes.

"For the train's steam whistle, the dryness or wetness of the steam affects the sound. Different locomotives also have different sounds. Some have a tiny single-note, a shriek and others, a larger plain one with deeper tones, and still others, a multi-chime one. The most popular is the three-note version.

"I think that most people like the train whistle but some complain about them since they carry for miles, especially on cold winter nights. But still some people do not hear them and run into trains or trains run into them. One has to measure the safety of the whistle against the harmful effects noise pollution might have on humans. But they do reduce accidents and improve safety. Some people, like me, even like the sound of a train whistle for it reminds me of steamboats and calliopes.

"What I find intriguing are the creative whistle codes that engineers use to communicate with other railroad workers or the public," Clarence continued. "Combinations of long and short whistles give specific meanings. Some give instructions, some a safety signal or movements of the train. Two longer sounds indicate that the train is releasing its brakes and is beginning to move, three short whistles mean the train is backing up; a long one and three short ones indicate a flagman should protect the rear of the train; two longs, a short and a long indicates the train is approaching a public grade crossing. So, you see, there are instructions in all of those toots."

Louie and David arrived in town and went immediately to the doctor's home which served as a clinic. David grimaced and almost fainted as Dr. Ogilvie stitched the loose skin together and put clamps in the larger area. A strapping was out of mind for both of them, and instead they visited a store nearby to buy a chocolate bar, with plenty of time to catch the train for home.

WATER WITCHING

Janos was a water witcher. He did not vaunt his power but every farm household knew he had it. When the water in the well on top of the hill near the family house was going dry, Louie enlisted Janos and his witching power to find another well. He took a forked willow branch, walked around the yard and soon found an empowering area at the bottom of the hill.

He admitted that he had not mastered the technique of calculating the energizing force to ascertain the depth of the water, nor did he use it for other projects, but admitted that something of note was there. Some regarded him as a kook but Louie was convinced of the value of this practical skill even though he did not possess it himself. He found water, a well driller was hired, dug 25 feet and indeed found abundant water.

Some individuals could divine for buried metals, gemstones, oil or even grave sites. Such practitioners used a dousing rod similar to Janos'. Louie was aware that scientists generally discredited this technique and attributed its positive results to the random chance of finding water in favorable terrain. According to these judgements, the stick which Janos used moved only because of his accidental or involuntary motion. In the 16th century, Martin Luther listed dowsing as an act that broke the first commandment by trusting in false gods, an act of occultism. Others called the action and results superstitious or satanic. But for the Anne-Louie household it was a blessing.

4-H CLUB

Although the minimum age for membership in the local 4-H Club was 12, Louie again tried his reasoning powers and argued that although his son was 10 years old, the age of 10 was close to 11, and 11 close to 12. The leader, Pete Schlitz, had no trouble with that type of logic. So, with agricultural fervor, David joined; it was the only social outing for him in town.

The 4-H Club's emblem was a four-leaf clover with an H on each leaf, standing for head, heart, hands and health. To begin each 4-H meeting, members recited the following together: I pledge my HEAD to clearer thinking, my HEART to greater loyalty, my HANDS to larger service, and my HEALTH to better living, for my club, my community, my country and my world. David was not sure what all of those lines meant, but everybody was reciting them. Its motto was Learn to Do by Doing. He heard that cowboy Roy Rogers was a member of this agricultural club in the States.

David welcomed mingling with fellow Club members, for they were generally not ones he associated with since they were not from his church or school, although a few of his relatives attended. The Club's activities were challenging: identifying weeds, and car and machinery parts, growing a plot of grain on four acres, keeping it free of weeds and cultivating a border around it, making a sign indicating one's name and the type of grain grown; displaying a grain sample at the annual local achievement day and at the Prince Albert Fair.

Each step in this 4-H project was important. Louie chose a plot of rich loam soil to plant Exeter oats. It grew to an extraordinary height so that parts of it lodged. David kept it looking clean by extracting wild oats and mustard weeds and by cultivating the border with his mother using a horse and hand cultivator.

Louie contacted the local commercial sign-making shop so that David could trace exact letters for his sign. He was rightly excited when the grain judge arrived to inspect his neatly kept plot and sign. The judge walked through it, examined the quality of the grain and took a photo of it.

During his first year as a Club member, David won first prizes for his plot, for his sign and for the grain sample. For this sample, he had used a tweezers and picked only the best kernels for presentation, only those kernels that were plump and without any hint of green colouring.

One of the 4-H Club's activities was the identification of motor vehicle and machinery parts; another was the identification and eradication of noxious weeds. While some of these invasive plants were beneficial, most of them could choke crops, pastures and native grassy areas. Pete provided books for members so they could study these various weeds.

One of these unwanted plants was hoary cress. Livestock usually did not eat this noxious weed. Once established, it was highly competitive, particularly with native vegetation on rangelands. It spread primarily by its root system. A perennial, its lower leaves were stalked and hairy while upper leaves clasped the stem and were usually hairless; numerous white flowers produced at the top of the plant gave rise to its other common name of white-top.

Another noxious weed that David studied was leafy spurge. It is also a perennial, spread by seeds but also has persistent vertical and horizontal underground root stocks on which it produces shoot buds. Extremely resilient, it reproduces primarily by re-sprouting from its extensive, persistent, creeping root system. Leafy spurge roots can extend laterally and to a great depth.

It can form dense stands over time and a large plant can produce up to 130,000 seeds. All parts of the plant contain a milky-coloured latex that can poison livestock and cause skin irritation on humans. Its numerous leaves are long, narrow, waxy, have smooth edges and are bluish-green in colour, turning yellowish or reddish-orange in late summer. Flowers are small and yellowish-green.

Purslane or portulaca has smooth, reddish, mostly prostrate stems and alternate leaves clustered at stem joints and ends. The yellow flowers have five regular parts. Purslane has a taproot with fibrous secondary roots and is able to tolerate poor, compacted soils and drought. As it then shrivels, it can survive between stones. Humans can eat it and it contains a wide array of vitamins and minerals.

The stems of toadflax are erect and hairless. Numerous leaves and bright yellow flowers are like a long spur extending from its base. These snapdragon-like flowers can have orange colouring on the throat. Farmers who placed a 45-gallon drum of soil over a plant found that it gradually penetrated it and rose to the top.

While identifying weeds, particularly the obnoxious ones, was a challenge, the 4-H Club provided discovery trips including one to the Annual Fair in Prince Albert and its Lund's Wild Life Exhibit, to its Penitentiary, and a tour of the Robin Hood Flour Mill in Saskatoon.

On one of these trips, David rode with the Schlitz family to Prince Albert. He remembers having to stop suddenly when one of the family members got car sick. On another occasion, an evening, Pete stopped the car as male occupants exited and gave as an excuse that they were watering the horse or catching a rabbit.

4-H members were given a tour of the Prince Albert Penitentiary, called the PA Pen, or just The Pen. As they visited the buildings and surroundings, they were surprised and a little aghast to learn that the 1921 site had a gallows and death row; it also had a 272-acre farm, a great enterprise for reforming prisoners who could take pride in their work while earning some cash. Women prisoners were originally housed here also but were moved to Battleford because of an influx of women prisoners resulting from the Doukhobor protests.

The Northern Tower of the facility is noteworthy, guide Leonard said. It consists of a well-proportioned, octagonal tower that features a concrete cornice and corbels, red brick veneer infill panels, and is capped with a one-story observation deck and security gallery. It commands a presence on the south bank of the North Saskatchewan River and is surrounded by agricultural lands and mixed-use buildings.

It is designed in the architectural tradition of castles and fortresses. The Northern Tower contributes to the identification of the penitentiary and makes it a familiar landmark within the city and the region. The Tower is a first line of defense in maintaining prison security through the provision of supervision and surveillance. For this, it has narrow, deeply inset windows and doorways that complement the three additional corner towers.

"The city of Prince Albert has mixed feelings of having the PA Pen," Leonard noted. "We ranked after Regina and Saskatoon in procuring important services: Regina got the Legislature, Saskatoon, the University, and we got the third choice, the Pen!"

In the city, 4-H members also visited Lund's Wild Life Exhibit, housed along the North Saskatchewan River in the downtown area. It had an extensive collection of North American wildlife displayed in their natural settings.

During another summer outing, members toured the Robin Hood flour mill in Saskatoon. While walking through the mill, David and male members of the Club took many snatches of bran from the exposed bags. When chewed, wheat grain formed gum that stretched and expanded into bubbles. But it also became a laxative and as a consequence, on their return home, the drivers had to stop their cars on the road as these devouring brats relieved themselves in nearby bushes.

At a winter meeting of the town's 4-H agricultural club, leader Pete ventured the topic of another summer vacation spot for its members. Uppermost in his mind and that of many of the parents was the town of Watrous, well, not really the town, but two attractions that held claim of fame: one was Watrous' mineral waters and its swimming pool, and the other, nearby, was the CBK radio transmitter building and tower.

Pete had print material on both of these sites and he challenged Club members to read about these places. One of the pamphlets stated this about the mineral waters:

"Take the waters. Don't fight it. Relax, and you really can float on your back and read a newspaper without getting it wet. The water is also very refreshing. The specific gravity of 1.06 (density compared to water) makes you buoyant and so very safe for swimming. Visitors take advantage of its buoyancy to do physiotherapeutic exercises that help ease aching joints.

"The temperature of the water is a factor affecting its salinity. The chemical properties of the water are unique. Little Manitou Lake has many of the same natural qualities as the Dead Sea in Palestine. It contains a lot of magnesium which is good for the skin and for bronchial passages and contains much iodine, which is beneficial for certain glandular functions. The minerals in the water make the colour look metallic bronze."

At the waters, nobody needed any persuasion about its benefits. For prairie people, the swimming pool was immediately attractive. David's rather corpulent uncle, Ben, rented a bathing suit and eagerly ventured into the waters. Aunt Anne, also corpulent, was shy and reluctant until she was persuaded to don one and plunge in also.

David remembered from the information he perused, that there really was no research data to prove the waters' healing qualities, but there were many medical claims about how good it is for conditions such as arthritis, rheumatism, and skin troubles (eczema and psoriasis). "If you have the slightest scratch or cut, one dip into the water makes the sore heal up really fast," the brochure stated.

The claims continued: Natural oils extracted from the lake were made into hair tonic and toothpaste. Residents harvested the mineral salts and sold them to drug stores across Saskatchewan. Mudpacks from the lake could be applied to sore muscles and joints. Although smallpox and other diseases brought by Europeans devastated Indians and their communities, Manitou Lake cured their rheumatic conditions and burning fevers. There were many more stories, one from the Assiniboine people:

In 1837 there was a smallpox epidemic. European and traditional Indian medicines provided no cure. When the Indians were fleeing from the plains to try to get away from the scourge, they passed the site of Lake Manitou. When two smallpox-affected young men in one group were unable to go any farther, they erected a small tent in which they could spend their remaining days.

After the rest of the tribe shunned them and departed, the young men were so consumed by thirst that they crawled to the shore of the lake nearby and, as well as drinking from Lake Manitou, they immersed themselves in the water. Apparently, it cooled their fever, and they spent the next few days on the beach, bathing in the waters. Within a few days they recovered and were able to take up the trail of their party. It was from this event that the Indians regarded the waters of Lake Manitou as having great therapeutic value.

Medicine men named the lake Manitou because of its likeness to the Great Spirit, Gitchi Manitou. It became known as the Lake of the Healing Waters, or the Lake of the Good Spirit. Warring tribes never carried on their feuds when visiting the lake but laid down their weapons before entering the water. Tribes from as far east as the Great Lakes and as far west as the Rockies came to the lake which became famous for healing.

David and fellow 4-H members learned from brochures that the water in the pool at Manitou Springs is channeled from Little Manitou Lake, and is then filtered, and cleaned. The pool enclosure has 98 individual cubicles, each with its own little door and mirror where you can change into your bathing suit. The pool's temperature is 80 degrees Fahrenheit. There is a sunlit fountain in the shallow end where a fine spray of fresh well-water spurts from its top.

There are diving boards, barrels, logs, and other platforms on which to play. The most spectacular thing at the pool is a trapeze with rings hanging from chains, five on one side and seven on the other. These present the challenge to grab one, swing, grab another, moving down the whole length and back. If you fall into the water, you were considered an amateur. What a wonderful playing area for David and the gang!

In the late summer afternoon, the 4-H Club and parents motored to the nearby CBC radio station and tower, known to them as CBK Watrous. Again, the visitors had examined print material and illustrations of this masterpiece on the Prairies. They learned that the Canadian Broadcasting Corporation opened this radio station on July 29, 1939 in order to add another voice to its cross-country radio broadcast network. CBK Radio 540 boomed onto the air with 50,000 watts of power.

There were several reasons why the area of Watrous was chosen as an ideal prairie location for this radio station: 1. the same highly conductive minerals as in Little Lake Manitou are found in the surrounding soil; 2. the local altitude and the flat land were excellent for radio transmission to the three prairie provinces; 3. since telephone connections were difficult, the site's nearness to a rail line and therefore to telegraph service ensured ready communication.

On the radio, 540 was near the bottom of the AM dial, a clear-channel station which had the highest protection from interference from other stations.

As the 4-H gang drove to the outskirts of Watrous, they noticed the 465-foot tower and a modern brick, tile and stucco building with blue trim. On its exterior in large blue letters, was C B K and in smaller ones, Canadian Broadcasting Corporation. A high chain fence surrounded the area.

As the 4-H Club members entered the building, they saw the studio operators in action; they seemed from another world as they sat with strange gadgets over their ears, surrounded by turntables and other weird things. The guide, Albert, gave a tour of the split-level air-conditioned building, its radio studios, an announcer's lounge, living quarters for the staff, and a heated two-car garage; the equipment took up two floors.

The complex had an underground fallout shelter in case of a nuclear attack for it was such an important communications site, Albert said, that armed guards protected the transmitter during World War II, closing it during part of the War. From these broadcasts, prairie people realized they were also standing on guard for their country as they followed the advance of allied and German and Italian troops. From broadcasts they learned of the general location of their loved ones and heard the dreaded words, missing and presumed dead.

Up to 12 people worked here. Of special interest was the large floor map of Canada showing CBC stations and private affiliates. The map was of inlaid battleship linoleum, 40 by 17 feet, with each province in alternating colours of buff and terracotta, and lakes, bays and oceans in mottled blue. Small black triangles marked the radio stations. Albert stated that CBK was the only CBC-owned outlet between Winnipeg and Vancouver. Its broadcast frequency gave it excellent primary coverage with reception as far away as New Zealand and Australia.

The K in the CBK call signal recalled the last name of Henry Kelsey, a Hudson Bay employee and, in 1691, the first recorded European to explore the Prairies. The station's two five-foot long vacuum tubes had water-cooled jackets using distilled water and at one time when the water pipeline broke, engineers used ice packs to cool the tubes.

Radiating from the tower base, like spokes from the hub of a wheel, were 120 wires each 500 feet long and buried under the earth, grounding the system and totaling 11 miles of copper wire.

Its first broadcast, in both English and French, featured prairie premiers, federal ministers and a tribute from the Happy Gang, a classic CBC variety show. During the War, telegrams arrived from Toronto and Winnipeg and were broadcast from here including that of Vera Lynn singing We'll meet again, a memorable song for the troops.

Mr. Schlitz, who liked to tell odd stories, said he heard the radio announcement, Canadian Broadcasting Corporation, many times, but one time it came out, Canadian Broadcorping Castration!

HUSH HUSH HOME BREW

The depression and post-depression years were very difficult. In order to survive, many farmers made and sold home brew; they needed the money to buy food. This brewing was an illegal act and the Royal Canadian Mounted Police searched for brewing stills. Sometimes the police found them, but owners often denied any association with brewing even if the still was on their property. However, if the home brewer was apprehended because his excuse was not believable, he was given a fine, but if he was unable to pay, he would have to go to jail.

The Anne-Louie family knew that Uncle Frank made home brew and that he worked by moonlight or lantern. In daylight hours, he ploughed the fields and got the hardware man to drop off a 45-gallon drum of gas in the field every week. Later, Uncle Frank knew that some gas was stolen since he found identifiable tracks near the drum.

At a dance, the thief asked to buy some moonshine. "I'd have to charge you for two," Uncle Frank responded jokingly. "One is for the whisky, the other is for the stolen gas." The thief protested, but paid the full amount and they parted amicably. Other neighbours would consider different options to repay stealing; they might even talk of fixing his clock to even the score.

Home brew making—there was much talk about it but most of it was hush hush. Why the secrecy? David wanted to know. What was involved in its making? So, he walked the two miles to Uncle Frank's home. Unshaven and in bib overalls, he was repairing his International truck, but he quickly abandoned that task when David indicated he wanted to know more about making hootch.

"I could talk endlessly about this fascinating job, well, not really a job, but a hobby of mine. Let's just get into the swing of things and see it in action. I'll show you where the still and distiller are, but you mustn't tell anyone," Uncle Frank said.

"I promise," David replied.

So, they hurriedly headed past the barn and onto a trail in the bush and then past a fence closed by a gate. As they walked and conversed, both of them exhibited a kindred spirit regarding this secret process. There were several reasons for this: One was that the procedure was illegal and it was exciting to do something you're not supposed to do. Another was that everything in the making involved various changes, the change of many ingredients into something new, the change of the makers into creators and providers, and, alas, the possible pickling of some imbibers into stupefied drunkards.

But also, the brewers could be snitched on, caught, had to appear in police court and be given the option of a fine or 30 days in jail. "A farmer and fellow hootcher went through this process and he chose jail," Uncle Frank stated. "It was hell, he told me, for he became mentally and emotionally sick in there. He said he would rather pay the fine next time!"

As they arrived at a mound covered with branches Uncle Frank said: "Since it is daylight, I can easily find where I hid my machines. Let me just pull off the branches so we can see the whole works. Bees, wasps, hornets and flies of all kinds like the ingredients I make and so we have to swish them off.

"I actually like to work under cover of darkness for you can never be too guarded. Then I have to use a flashlight or bring my truck over here and use its headlights. Or the moon gives me a lot of light and after all that is why we call it moonshine. What I need is enough light to make my work easy and enough darkness to make my operation secure."

David thought it was fitting that Uncle Frank took to this clandestine trade for he was a natural tinkerer and hobbyist, often helping his family and friends. He liked to call his finished product, *hausgemacht,* homemade. Uncle Frank was really a generous sort, for he rarely sold his unlawful stuff but instead gave it away, bartered it for services or traded it for vegetables.

Although the ethics of making home brew was questionable, Uncle Frank tried to ascertain how his product would be properly used before he parted with it. He was loathe to give it to alcoholics for they would abuse it, nor did he make it available for barn dances, nor give it to those who would make a lot of profit reselling it.

"I like the idea of hiding from the police while making moonshine. I suppose it shows my long-time rebellious spirit, but I also like to think it shows that I am my own boss. I think I am in the right, for I am a private person doing it on my own property. I have a God-given right to do so," he said in self-justification. "Here I am making good stuff and not relying on businesses to make it and sell it at a high price. Like the Germans, us Hungarians consider making wine and home brew as part of who we are. If we lose this right, we are no longer Hungarians; we lose our culture."

Uncle Frank gave examples of other practitioners: "I read that in the last century a lot of whisky traders came from the United States to Alberta to sell the stuff in exchange for furs. A vat containing it was set in a beer parlor and snuffers there regularly spit into it, making it more colourful, and powerful, I guess. Those whisky traders also watered down this hootch and sometimes put arsenic poisoning into it to give it a sharper taste. Not too much of that for it would kill the customers. I don't do any of that.

"Now to the real making of the liquor. You see this big pot. I put potatoes, raisins, prunes and yeast into it—anything that will ferment. I check it after a while as it bubbles and boils; then I strain it and let it ferment some more. I check it again and notice large amounts of protein, fat, and inactive yeast on the bottom of the pot. So, I leave this sediment there and take off the liquid, strain it again and place it in a second container. This beverage must be kept at a stable temperature ranging from 64 to 75 degrees Fahrenheit."

Despite his unkempt exterior, Uncle Frank demonstrated that he was not a sloppy but a careful and concerned brewer: "I make sure all my equipment is clean and I use the best water. Some use car or tractor radiators for this distilling, but there is a danger of poisoning the stuff and causing blindness in the drinkers, so I shy away from that.

"Then I heat this beverage in my distiller. It comes out in drips from this steam system. I add syrup colouring to make it look and taste better. It costs me next to nothing. At first it was awful stuff, but now that I have more experience, I think it is excellent."

"Brewing seems like a lot of hard work. Do you ever make mistakes?" David asked.

"Making this beverage is like making bread," Uncle Frank answered. "Some turns out really good; some gets burnt; some doesn't rise and some you eat only because you don't want to offend the baker; if it is dry, you force it down and almost choke. Making moonshine is like baking bread; both take practice and some failures before you come up with something you'd want to share."

There was no stopping Uncle Frank as he eagerly carried on. "I throw away a few ounces of the first distilled stuff. In that way I remove any poisonous material; this also increases its strength. A fellow moonshiner asked me if I could drink one of his best batches. I had to try it and not be too critical. It had a nice colour but it looked a little filthy. I drank as little as possible and as it went down, I closed my nose and prayed; it was terrible. A saying came to mind that making whisky or brandy is not hard, but making something you'd want to drink, well, that took some practice. On another occasion, I drank some that looked like sludge or mud. It had a sour taste and a foul smell like lye soap."

"Don't people get drunk even with your good stuff?" David again questioned.

"One of my friends told me that he didn't care how it looked as long as it was alcohol. If it had in addition a pleasant taste that was a bonus. After drinking a lot of it, he said, 'Sometimes I see two moons. And sometimes I don't see any moons at all. What the hell, what's wrong with a good old-fashioned hangover?'

"Well, I hope that people feel good when they drink my brewing, but they should still do it in moderation as they do with other things. So, I test both how strong the stuff is and how healthy it is. I put some of it in a clean jar and shake it. If large bubbles form and burst in a short time, then I know I have some tough stuff. If smaller bubbles form and disappear more slowly, then it has lower alcohol.

"But a more common test for its proof or strength is to pour a small amount into a spoon and set it on fire. Safe and strong stuff burns with a blue flame; one that is unhealthy burns with a yellow or reddish flame and then moonshiners can be wary, for the saying is that red is dead."

Uncle Frank then recalled a time when not everyone thought that liquor was a good thing. "There was a period in Canada and the U.S. history when possessing alcohol was prohibited. Do you know that the city of Saskatoon was founded by Temperance settlers who believed in banning alcohol altogether? This is no longer the case here, but there are still some hangups about alcohol.

"As you know, I am for the easy making and free use of alcohol, for a good drink can be heavenly. Those promoting prohibition, or dries as they were called, thought that alcohol led to wife-beating and abuse of children. They thought that outlawing alcohol would eliminate corruption and lead to sober politics. These dries didn't really know the benefits of a good drink. Obviously, I am in favor of the wets instead."

Uncle Frank told a few funny stories about home brew. One farmer made many trips to town with his truck but always had a bull or cow in the truck box. He used the animal as a decoy so that attention was not drawn to the brew but to the animal in the box.

Another farmer carried a Roman collar on the seat of his car; he put the collar on whenever trouble was near. Even the local pastor had sympathy for the moonshiners for they shared their best stuff with him. One time an assistant pastor helped out in the parish but was puzzled about what type of penance he should give to those who confessed to making hootch. "What penance to give him?" the pastor advised, "if it's good stuff, give him five dollars!"

David ascertained that Uncle Frank had read and thought a lot about his hobby. "Actually, a lot of corruption came in with prohibition," he continued. "I read in *The Western Producer,* that a gangster named Al Capone had a hangout in Moose Jaw and put half of Chicago's police force on his payroll. Moose Jaw became a hub for Capone's rumrunners and gangsters; the city tunnels became warehouses for illegal alcohol which was shipped on the Soo Line to the United States. Gangsters got rich and violent as they fought over control of liquor sales and promoted prostitution and gambling.

"In the *Producer* I read a cute poem from these prohibition days. I memorized it:

> Mother's in the kitchen
> Washing out the jugs;
> Sister's in the pantry
> Bottling the suds;
> Father's in the cellar
> Mixing up the hops;
> Johnny's on the front porch
> Watching for the cops.

"But generally, you were safe from the law if you brewed or distilled in your own home," Uncle Frank said. "But if you did it outside, the Mounties might find you and bust you. A home is all right, but you need quite a bit of space and the continuous smell might turn a lot of people off."

Again, Uncle Frank had recourse to history: "There are many stories about the positive use of alcohol. Monasteries in Europe distilled it and pharmacists and doctors used it for medicine. Early Europeans in Canada used it as a trade item with the Indians; firewater, they called it, for it often led to uncontrolled actions."

Uncle Frank concluded his animated and detailed narrative: "I don't see why home brewing is immoral. I am just an amateur, perfecting my art. Maybe someday when I have a really good batch, I'll send a bottle or two to our top boss: 'Here's to you, Mr. Prime Minister! Taste and see how good it is. And it is from the Prairies.'"

"I hope our leader will appreciate your good drink," David affirmed.

TURKEYS AND CHICKENS

Anne took pride in her large flock of turkeys. She had gently nourished them when they were cute chicks and now they were fat and strolled freely in the yard. Come Christmas time, many households liked to have a turkey for their festive meal.

The Louie-Anne family was happy to provide a nice heavy bird. The turkeys had to be killed, bled and plucked before they were sold and delivered. They heard a story that one bird who had gone through this process, erected herself, stepped off the table, and proceeded to walk about stark naked and certainly not dead. Loud screams ensued and the farmer was summoned to kill the bird again.

David was a prankster, especially when he had the help of other boys his age. He was always into mischief. One time when his parents were not home, he decided to see what their flock of turkeys would do if they were given a good drink of homemade chokecherry wine. He wanted to see the reaction of the prominent gobbler especially, one who took a dislike to him.

So, David scooped a batch of chop, that is, ground up grain, and mixed it with this wine. It must have had a good taste because the turkeys quickly gobbled it up. When David's parents came home and saw the turkeys staggering and acting ever so strange, they immediately suspected David was up to something. Needless to say, David found it very uncomfortable to sit still for a few days.

On another occasion, David persuaded Theresa to help him catch a bunch of chickens and stuff them in an old heater. They packed in five or ten of them. Then David decided it was time to take them out. The first few came out and took off running, the second ones were a little slower on the take off, but the last ones didn't move and they had to put them down.

"We'd better tell Mom about these," David said to Theresa. Mom nearly had a heart attack when she saw her chickens lying dead. She suspected a prankster operation, elicited a confession, gave her children a good tongue lashing, decided to bury the dead birds and not tell Louie.

MILKING THE COWS

David often helped his mother with milking the cows in the evening. On this Saturday, she completed most of this chore, but then went inside the house to prepare supper. She asked David and Theresa to finish the milking task. They hurried to the barn and without their mother's strength and proficiency managed to procure a pail of milk. They really wanted to complete the task quickly so they could go to town early in the evening.

While they were not guarding the pail of milk, a calf, loose in the barn, drank most of it. What to do? They went to the well and pumped a liberal amount of water so that the pail seemed reasonably full. They were afraid to tell their mother of the event for she might accuse them of carelessness and not let them go to town that evening.

When they processed the diluted milk through the separator, Anne was puzzled why it produced so little cream. She was certain something was wrong with the cows. So instead of putting this diluted cream into storage in the ice house, she poured it into the skim milk pail and fed it to the calves. With their allowance of 25 cents, they went to town.

COOL ICE HOUSE

Since the family did not initially have a major source of electricity, they did not own a refrigerator or a freezer. Instead, they had an ice house. It was a low-slung structure hidden among bushes and trees, accessed by interior steps, and close to their home. For its cooling operation, in the spring, Louie and David cleaned the hollowed underground site from old sawdust and then used a double box wagon to haul large amounts of snow to fill the cavity, snow that was not too laden with water, for that ice was already somewhat melted. Other farmers cut ice blocks and used them instead of snow.

The operation of sawing wood in the late fall provided a lot of sawdust. Louie spread this on top of the snow as an insulator to slow the melting during the summer. The family used this hideaway mostly to store cream; to do this, they hollowed out an area in the sawdust, dug into the snow and inserted the ice cream can and spread the sawdust around it. Beer, milk, butter and meat were also kept there. Once a small pig wandered into this cool place, managed to lift the cream can lid and had a delicious meal. In the morning, Louie found him drowned in the can. "The thief got what he deserved," he remarked.

Some residents in town had an icebox in their kitchens. This wooden box lined with tin was a handy apparatus but required periodic restocking of ice. As a transition from ice houses and ice boxes to freezers and refrigerators, a neighbouring town had a locker plant housing refrigerator units. Families could rent one in which to keep frozen items. With its butcher shop, this business offered meat processing and sale of local products. An inconvenience was that one had to drive to this shop periodically to pick up frozen items. These shops became relatively obsolete with the advent of electricity and freezers and refrigerators.

QUEEN LIKES JUNE BERRIES

In late June or early July, Anne, David and Theresa went to pick june berries, also called saskatoons. Their farm was surrounded with many berry bushes and relatives and neighbours felt free to pick themwithout permission. Some berries were on high bushes, others on low. During some years, they were plentiful, during others they were scarce. Sometimes they were as big as fingernails, sometimes they were small as pin cherries. But they were always delicious and gave of the abundance they had.

When the family bushes were stripped of berries, the family went elsewhere, also picking without permission. One farmer was very protective of his fields and while the Anne-Louie family was picking and making a lot of sounds in jubilation, he showed up, told them that they were trespassing and confiscated the berries. They were in shock, but returned the next day, continued to pick in the area and remained quiet and picked twice as much.

At home the family cleaned the berries from stink bugs, twigs, leaves and shriveled berries and then served themselves an ample amount with cream. They thought it was the most delicious fruit imaginable. Anne made jams and jellies from the berries so they lasted for the whole year. Anne heard that Canada's queen ate june berry pie when she visited. She was so delighted that she insisted on taking back home several pies and vowed to do so when she visited again. The berries were a great gift for everyone, including royalty!

RATIONING FOR THE WAR

People in prairie cities complained about rationing during the war, but those on farms had their own produce such as meat, eggs, vegetables and fruit. Some of it was eaten directly from the garden and it was good and fresh while others were canned in sealers for meals during the winter and spring.

Yes, during the war there was rationing of gasoline, especially if it was used for recreational purposes. Farmers had an exemption, for their gas was cheaper to purchase, designated by its purple colouring. The temptation was to use this less expensive type not only for tractors and trucks, for which it was designated, but also for cars. The police checked vehicles for purple gas; if it was used, there was a fine or imprisonment.

The family heard about skimping on butter but they had lots of cream to make it. They had to rely on coupons to purchase limited amounts of sugar and coffee. Clothes were expensive and in short supply so Anne made dresses from flour sacks, and soap from animal fat. They noticed that there was no nickel or chrome on machinery and vehicles, for these flashy items were used for the war effort. Some farmers found it difficult if not impossible to pay their taxes so they earned a meager income by working on public jobs such as hauling gravel, digging for culverts or cutting brush to build roads.

While Hungarians were delighted with poppies and used them to make poppy bread, some people connected the seeds with the drug, opium. The family did not know anyone who abused these seeds but some relatives who had a number of sons joked about this. Their home faced their large garden that grew poppy plants. Despite repeated calls from their mother to wake up in the morning, they delighted in continuing to sleep and used the excuse that they were drugged by the poppies that wafted their odor into their bedroom.

Since many commodities were in short supply during the war, the government campaigned to save and reuse vital materials. Small towns held drives, collecting scrap paper so it could be used for packing around equipment and weapons. They collected all kinds of metal to be recycled to make war vehicles and bombs. Since copper was needed, they saved pennies to be melted down. These drives generated a strong sense of community and the patriotic feeling that everyone was helping in the war effort.

During the Second World War, Canadians became accustomed to this rationing; the government forced them to use ration books issued by The Wartime Prices and Trade Board. Citizens had to submit coupons from these books in order to purchase commodities designated as scarce. Each book had a specific number, name and address with telephone number if available. There were ration coupons for meat, preserves, tea or coffee, sugar, cheese, jam, and margarine.

Ration books were in both languages and not transferable; their holders had the responsibility to detach a coupon only in the presence of the supplier or his representative. Penalties for violations were $5,000 or imprisonment or both, but these varied.

Later The Food Conservation Committee of the Government of Canada issued a basic handbook, Food is Everybody's Business, to justify past practices, especially rationing. One section in its 32 pages was entitled, Canada's Armed Forces Must be Fed . . . and Well Fed! This section was based on the axiom that an army marches on its stomach. "If anyone must have enough food and proper food, it is the fighting man. . . . The man in training needs a more liberal diet than the average civilian and the Standard Ration is worked out carefully on that premise."

Besides rationing items for the war effort, the federal government sold war bonds. Purchasers could buy, for instance, a $100 bond at a discount, say $75, and then redeem it at full value when the bond matured. War bonds appealed to a sense of patriotism and conscience. One advertisement to purchase bonds featured a stylish young woman against a bright red background. She wore a large flowered hat, had ribboned pigtails, pearls and many bracelets; as she glanced at herself in a hand-held mirror, her long, flowing upheld skirt revealed high heels.

The ad read: for when tomorrow comes, Canada Savings Bonds on sale today for cash or easy installments. Another ad appealed to rural investors: A hatted farmer in suspenders grasped a sheaf of wheat alongside a woman holding a hen and a young boy with a piglet: Buy Victory Bonds with cash and produce.

CATECHISM CLASSES

Although all children who came to the Stearns public school were from Roman Catholic families, this school was no longer a strictly Catholic one for it was now within one of the Saskatchewan school districts. Nevertheless, this school enrolled in a Roman Catholic catechism correspondence course. The handouts had illustrations for each lesson printed on newsprint. Students read the material and answered the questions which were sent for correction to the Sisters in Bruno who had created the program.

There was another form of religious instruction and that was the catechism classes in church conducted each summer. Theresa and David travelled there, a 10-mile round trip by horse and cart. They met children from their own school, but also from surrounding rural schools. They purchased a catechism for their age group, a green-covered Baltimore Catechism which indicated they were older students.

A short, stocky, bald-headed priest, Father Bernard, greeted the children and sat on top of the front bench facing them. When he read the Bible, the heroes came alive and were right in the room. Although David couldn't always understand the pastor's English (someone said he knew five languages and spoke all of them at the same time!), he asked pupils to open the catechism and memorize the answers. On the basis of this kind of knowledge, pupils could receive First Communion, Confirmation and Solemn Communion. During these ceremonies, he frequently inserted his own name with that of the child on the relevant certificates, reasoning that "Bernard is a great name."

David and Theresa remember their catechism lessons. The first one was On the End of Man. Most of the pupils already knew the answers to questions like Who made the world? Why did God make you? What must we do to save our souls? The correct answer was that "to save our souls, we must worship God by faith, hope, and charity; that is, we must believe in Him, hope in Him, and love Him with all our heart."

To the question, "How shall we know the things which we are to believe?" the answer was "We shall know the things which we are to believe from the Catholic Church, through which God speaks to us."

David was quite attentive and credulous. Several boys created minor disturbances by poking each other and telling jokes. Father Bernard massaged his snuff-stained moustache and intervened to restore order. Then he snorted the snuff into his bandanna handkerchief.

At recess time, pupils played tag in the shade of the large church, for it was generally hot outside. Then they ate their lunch. Afterwards they went to the vicinity of the horse barns at the base of the hill on which the church stood. They found tangy gooseberries and scrumptious wild strawberries.

For the most part, the boys and girls did not question the catechism answers publicly, but took them on faith. Some of the questions and answers were not very clear, such as, Why can there be but one God? The answer was There can be but one God, because, God, being supreme and infinite, cannot have an equal. And, of course, the riddle of the trinity, three persons in one God, really distinct, and equal in all things.

There were some intriguing things: Adam and Eve being innocent and holy when created, but becoming unfaithful to God's commands and eating the forbidden fruit. Here was something frightful about their sin for they were doomed to misery and death and we also inherited their sin and punishment.

It was really hard to tell the difference between original sin and actual sin for both were sins. It was also hard to know what actual sin was like, for it included sins of thought, word, deed and omission. Sinful thoughts were not easy to understand for one could have all kinds of thoughts.

There were such big words: the seven capital sins of pride, covetousness, lust, anger, gluttony, envy, and sloth. Some pupils confused these with the seven gifts of the Holy Ghost for both were seven.

A puzzling question was, Did anything remain of the bread and wine after their substance had been changed into the substance of the body and blood of our Lord? And the answer was, After the substance of the bread and wine had been changed into the substance of the body and blood of our Lord, there remained only the appearances of bread and wine. But certainly, the host still looked like bread. Adding to the puzzle was the big word, transubstantiation to indicate the change of the bread and wine into the body and blood of Jesus.

A hard teaching was the necessity for a fast before Communion. The answer was, The fast necessary for Holy Communion is to abstain from all food, beverages, and alcoholic drinks from midnight on. That was a long time! Water could be taken at any time.

The church had a cemetery across from the school where during the summer, snakes found a haven to sun themselves against the tombstones. When catechism goers visited there, they spied some large green and black ringed ones that appeared very dangerous. Daring boys caught them and played with them. I

In the far corner of the cemetery, by the road, there was a grave of a man who had committed suicide. David's heart thumped very hard as he ran fast or backward past this grave site, but all of a sudden, some of the bigger boys who had hidden themselves in the bush came out and frightened him almost to death.

3

School

THE TEACHER

David noticed someone walking toward his home in late summer. It was neighbour Lucy and she had come to tell Anne that school would begin in two weeks and that this Saturday afternoon there would be an acquaintance time for new parents and students. Lucy, a senior student at Stearns School, invited David to be there. Louie dropped the two off that Saturday. Teacher, Miss Schmidt welcomed them.

She was a young, small, cheerful and likeable person. After completing her high school, she went to Normal School and learned that she should not smile or laugh for the first six months of the school year. Instead, she should lay down the law and make sure that she was in charge, that she was the boss. She should be fierce and win her pupils' obedience.

David's mother was in great admiration of the teacher. Although she was born and brought up on a nearby farm, Miss Schmidt had an ambition to go to Normal School and then the daring to teach in a country school. Since there was no teacherage on the school grounds, she had to board at a rural household which had no running water or inside toilet. She became one with that family, however. She had to put in long class preparation hours and walk in the cold and snow to get a ride in a passing caboose. In her boarding place, she had little privacy, was isolated, and had to contend with flies and mosquitoes.

On her first day of school, Miss Schmidt thought of doing an experiment. She mingled with the big boys before the school began. They thought she was one of the older girls. The boys shared plans on how to play tricks on the new teacher. When the teacher left the group and rang the bell to begin the school day, the boys realized that their cover had been blown; their faces turned red but Miss Schmidt merely smiled at them. She never had any trouble with those boys during the school year.

On that first day, children examined every detail of the teacher: her clothes, hair, shoes and nails. "When I returned their gaze," Miss Schmidt stated, "their peering eyes closed and sheepishly they turned in another direction. When their eyes opened again, I gave them a sly smile."

She must have been a dreamer to take on the responsibility for almost everything in the school: water, library, few textbooks, book of registry. She had to be inventive and resourceful: she noted the irregular attendance and the difficulty some pupils had in understanding the English language. She had to assume varied roles: diagnose illnesses, administer first aid, be a janitor, play and umpire games, settle disputes, ensure cleanliness, food, fair play and be knowledgeable in all the topics to teach: literature, arithmetic, history, correctness of speech, songs. She often bought prizes and goodies for her pupils.

Miss Schmidt had to discern and adjust to the temperament of the district. This rural district was generally laidback, but friendly nevertheless, industrious and religious. She had a special place in the district; she had to dress modestly but in some ways set the standard and be an example for the area.

Residents were very considerate of her, helpful and thoughtful, treating her as one of their own children, in an almost paternal and maternal manner. A parent sent a mustard plaster to her when she had a cold. On one occasion, she loaned her new dress to an older pupil for a special dance; on another occasion a bridesmaid asked to borrow it.

Stearns was a multi-graded school, eight grades plus a correspondence course for grade nine. It was demanding to maintain such a heavy schedule week in and week out. There was a set schedule: morning classes and study until 10:30, then a half hour recess. Time for noon lunch, with a recess until 1 pm; then a brief common and private reading time; another recess and then further study.

There was an emphasis on deportment, punctuality, good work habits and conduct; a grade determined standing in class and a record of number of times when late, days absent.

Pupils had to recite poetry learned by memory; they called it learning by heart. It was daunting to stand before the class and recite a certain section, but most pupils gained confidence in themselves by doing so. David loved reading and continued at home for the teacher gave him, for transporting her to school, the books *Treasure Island* and *Gulliver's Travels.*

Drilling focused on spelling, grammar, and the times tables. For tests pupils did a lot of cramming which resembled the process of stuffing a Christmas turkey. They poured facts into their heads and held them long enough to regurgitate them for the tests.

One Saturday Miss Schmidt drove with the hosting farmer to the neighbouring town. While shopping she met a male teacher and was happy, well mostly, to listen to his experiences. Norman said he was making $45 a month from which he had to pay room and board. He saved enough, however, to buy a new suit, for his present one was frayed and old looking. After all, the school inspector was coming soon and he had to look his best.

In great detail, Norman told her that he searched the Eaton's fall and winter catalogue and found a popular-style, all-wool suit for young men. It was hand finished, navy serge, strongly sewn, with good linings and linen canvass front, two-buttons with peak lapels. It included a double-breasted vest and 22-inch cuff bottom pants. Price, Cash on Delivery, $11.95.

"For its style and worth it was of downright good value," Norman reflected. "I thought how handsome, impressive and distinguished looking I would be in debuting it in school. But no, I waited until a social evening instead. It was an instant success as I received so many compliments on my natty appearance. All the girls wanted to dance with me while the boys avoided me.

"At end of the party, I decided to hang around since the women were cleaning up; one of them asked me to go into the dark and get some wood to stock the box. As I was gingerly but proudly bringing in an armful, a parent with a dishpan of sloppy water threw it out the door and hit me. There was screaming and great consternation. A parent dropped a plate and saucer which smashed. They gazed at me in horror and daubed my face, nose and hair with tea towels and sponged my suit. I was in a bit of a shock but appreciated all the attention. In the end, my appearance was much the same as before."

Miss Schmidt asked each child to bring something of interest to class and have a discussion about it. Some brought stones with fossil remains, animal bones, embroidery and crotcheting works. Less appealing were skulls of animals with fur and teeth. David brought a buffalo skeleton which he found near a summer Indian encampment and on the shore of their small lake.

When she went to Normal School, Miss Schmidt heard many horror stories about teachers and their pupils, some stories involving rural schools. In one narrative, a 14-year-old had emptied the water cooler, the only water supply, seemingly on purpose. This teacher asked him to put out the palms of his hands so that she could whack him. Instead, he pulled his hands away. The prescription then was to double the whacks. The added hits were ineffectual for the boy had hard calluses on his hands, but his wrists were sensitive, so there she went. The result was that her arm got weak and he went away bawling

Teachers hoped that parents would agree with the discipline they enforced in school. This was often the case, and when parents learned that their children were strapped in school they were strapped again at home. Such reinforcement tactics helped engrain a spirit of obedience in pupils.

But there were different parental responses. Miss Schmidt heard that a male teacher who had strapped a husky farm boy, took refuge in fear under his own desk as the boy's peers attacked him. After some time, the teacher emerged and expelled the perpetrator from the class, but his father promptly called a meeting of the trustees of which he was a member. He explained that the strapping had enhanced his son's image among his peers and his father was proud of his son since he displayed a promising sign of early manhood. His argument was persuasive and his son was promptly reinstated.

Some children were relatively well-behaved at home, but rascals at school. Others did all kinds of pranks at home and also misbehaved at school; they were consequently disciplined both at home and at school. Pupils could act in many creative and destructive ways. School penalties were meted out for fighting, refusing to do school work, playing hookey, forging report cards, throwing snowballs, doing damage to school property, manipulating and defying authority, swearing, disturbing the classroom, stealing, unchaste actions and remarks, cheating, tardiness, barn and outhouse shenanigans, cruelty to man and beast, smoking, lying, bullying, verbal attacks, sarcasm, unfavorable personal references, and belittling.

Punishments included detentions, writing out lines, pulling by the ears or hair, slapping or striking, hitting with rulers, pointers, books, pieces of chalk, blackboard erasers, smacks on the rear end, cuffs on the ear, hard thumps on the shoulders, grabbing by the shoulder and setting them down in their desk.

There was the strap for major offenses. Teachers used a piece of leather 15 inches long and two wide. It was stored in the teacher's desk drawer for handy use, beside the Department of Education School Register. Everyone knew where it was and it had the habit of disappearing for short periods of time.

There were many stories within the rural community from which budding teachers could learn. Boys in a neighbouring school were very unruly. They had heard on the radio that the allies during World War II had sentenced Nazi war criminals to the death penalty. These boys decided to enact a similar procedure at school. So, at recess time they grabbed a few of the younger boys, put nooses on their necks and hanged them on the basement rafters. They did this mostly to scare them, but ceased when one of the boys turned blue and the teacher and parents had to be summoned. The trustees expelled these perpetrators from school.

Miss Schmidt was determined to learn from the reported disciplinary actions. Before the beginning of the school year, she visited her boarding place and then contacted some of the older girls and asked them to help her call on the parents and talk to them about possible disciplinary problems. She learned that two 14-year-old boys, one of whom was still in Grade 3, were bigger and stronger than she was. But Miss Schmidt prepared herself psychologically for she had heard that teachers would almost be eaten alive and that children would see how far they could go in challenging authority.

GETTING TO SCHOOL

For $15, Louie purchased another horse named Lady, a strong one he rescued from becoming horsemeat for minks. Many farmers felt sorry to surrender their horses in this fashion for they had given many years of faithful service. David called Lady a plug for she was so slow. He made endless complaints about this to his father who then purchased a peppy one, Buddy, one with which he had three runaways.

In spring and fall he drove to the rural school in a cart, pulled by a single horse. On the seven-mile round trip, he often shared lunches;

well, maybe Theresa was forced to share some of hers. Theresa and David were driving their cart contentedly to school one autumn morning when a rather slow-moving John Deere D tractor passed them. The tractor's put put sound spooked Buddy and he lurched ahead, easily passing the tractor. David tried to contain him and tightened his hold on the reins but Buddy pulled the cart even faster. "What can I do to stop him?" David questioned in panic. "With great speed, we turned the corner into the school yard and I directed him toward the barn door. He ground to a halt and I breathed a sigh of relief."

On another occasion, David persuaded his Dad to use their luxury buggy instead of the cart to go to school. In it, passengers sat higher and since it had better springs they luxuriated in a smoother ride. He was persuasive and they drove off in Cadillac style. During their trip home, David thought Buddy was going too slow so he took out his trusty whip and slashed it on Buddy's rear. He jumped, tore the tugs, broke the single tree and ran home, while the buggy careened on the shoulder of the road and sailed into the ditch, still upright. Dejected, embarrassed, they were shaken up, but laughed and walked the last mile home.

Driving to school in winter time presented several challenges. Louie told David never to turn into the deep snow in order to let another caboose pass. "They have two horses instead of one and know how to control them in the snow. Also, let the teacher walk to the main road where you pick her up. Don't drive in to meet her."

It started to melt during this March winter and many farmers hired a caterpillar tractor with a snow plow to clear the roads and their driveways so they could drive their cars instead of their cabooses. As David and Theresa were driving to school, they stopped in the driveway of the teacher's boarding house. They waited and waited, but she did not walk out. So, David decided to drive in and fetch her. The caboose strode the plowed embankment, teetered sideways and fell on its side. Buddy panicked and tore the under part, the sleigh, from the caboose and galloped to school.

There were Theresa and David sandwiched in the interior on top of the hot stove. They emerged through the back door, puzzled but unhurt, as the boarding house owner arrived. He hitched his own horses and drove the three of them to school, put the sleigh and caboose together, fetched Buddy and things were normal again. No more active fetching of the teacher.

Each morning in spring, summer and fall, David fed and watered his horse, garbed him in harness, and then maneuvered him between the cart's two shafts. He put an oat sheaf in the back of the cart for Buddy's daytime nourishment. At first, hitching the horse was too great a task for a six-year-old alone, and Louie helped him each morning. At school, the older boys aided him to unhitch Buddy as he arrived, put him in the barn and give him the sheaf of oats. These boys again helped David hitch the horse to the cart at the end of the school day.

At home and in preparation for David's first day of school, Anne ordered an overall pants with its usual bib, and two shirts from the Eaton's catalogue. She took him to Pongracz's store in the neighbouring town to try on and purchase a new jacket.

On that first day, Louie drove him to school with their small truck. For David, the one-room school was a mysterious experience. He was bashful for he did not know anyone at school, well almost no one; in the cloakroom, he noticed the neighbour's wee girl who was younger than himself.

He felt a kindred spirit with her and with hesitant words asked her how come she was also beginning school. "My older brothers are here and I was the only one left at home and I wanted to come with them." As good a reason to come to school as any, David thought.

School felt like a foreign country, with no siblings or relatives, a strange atmosphere and a language he did not know very well. Standing on the upper stairs of the open door, Miss Schmidt welcomed him, showed him an individual slot for his lunch kit, and a hanger for his clothes.

Since David now knew the way to school, he could easily walk there. This time, as he approached the Wegleitner driveway, children in their car recognized him, stopped and picked him up. Otherwise, for the first month David walked the seven-mile round trip. He sometimes forgot his mittens and protected his hands from the cold with a handkerchief, a mandatory item for school. He passed through the school's wide steel gate now limping from the pupils' swinging weight.

David had seen the classroom before but this time he felt the impact of it. There were desks in rows like railroad cars he had seen in town; they were factory-made, with a hardwood top supported on a couple of iron frames like sewing machines. These tops had a large, smooth writing surface, with a pencil trough and a two-inch oval opening in the upper-right hand corner to hold a chrome-plated inkwell; desks had hinged lids which snapped shut with a click. Somebody's initials were inscribed faintly on his desk's surface. There was storage space underneath and a hard, hinged seat to be folded up at the end of the school day.

The smaller and younger pupils were seated on the left side of the classroom and the older ones on the right. Children were talking and walking around when all of a sudden everyone went to their desks and sat down. He did the same, the first time he had to imitate the conduct of others. Someone was in front of him, and someone behind him. But pupils sat for a long time.

There was a big blackboard in the front which ran the full width of the room. It had white markings on it and some drawings. Miss Schmidt wrote her name on this black wall and some other things David could not read. Then she took a piece of wood with felt on it and erased it. This was all very neat.

She asked one grade at a time to come to the blackboard, put questions to them and they had to put the right answers on the board. Then she went to another grade and meanwhile the pupils at the blackboard started playing tic-tac-toe or just doodled.

Miss Schmidt used a hectograph process to duplicate sheets of paper for colouring and information. The process was a little messy for it involved placing a master sheet with purple ink on a gelatin surface and pressing paper against it. Presto, the image was transferred to a paper copy. When this process was completed for her limited number of pupils, she soaked the gelatin with spirits, sponged the ink away and the pad was clean for the next master.

Paper was expensive so Miss Schmidt used the hectograph process only for special occasions such as Christmas and Easter, and for art purposes although she preferred the pupils creating original coloured works rather than merely filling in the outlined forms.

After a while David got tired of sitting and decided to get up and walk around. Miss Schmidt asked him what he was doing. He felt very sheepish; she stated that everyone was to remain seated until there was a break. He was mystified by pupils who raised their hands and noticed that the teacher nodded in approval; they then disappeared only to reappear. He thought he would try it myself. Up went his hand. A nod. Now what? He wandered about the cloakroom and then returned perplexed to his desk.

Miss Schmidt then made an announcement that anyone who had to go to the toilet had to put up his hand and ask to leave the room. Sometimes she was either busy or grumpy and ignored the wildly waving hand; an accident once occurred as the pupils were about to be dismissed for the day;

she peed on the floor, cried and was very embarrassed; this was followed by endless peer teasing.

Then Miss Schmidt initiated another rule: if a pupil wanted to sharpen a pencil, he held up a pencil; if he wanted to go to the toilet, he held up two fingers and Miss Schmidt nodded her head and went on with the class. The only one who could exit the classroom without any form of permission was the one in charge of fueling the furnace. Now the raising of hands and extension of fingers made sense to David.

During the first break some pupils went to a strange container and took the cup beside it, put it under a silver spout, pushed a button and out came some water. Again, this was very neat.

While looking around, David spied a new, blue-bound hard covered book. He asked permission to take it in hand and although he could not read it very well, he liked its royal blue cover, delighted in opening it, smelling its newness and gently paging through it. He asked Miss Schmidt whether he could take it home.

"Yes, you can," she said, "but take good care of it."

"Thank you. I will cover it so it will not become messy," he promised. At home, Anne encased it with a brown paper cover and kept it free from any moisture or food.

David quickly opened its pages again, and since Anne had already tutored him in the letters of the alphabet, he followed them, now placed in rows with illustrative pictures. He felt proud to have such a book in his hands and turn its pages by himself. Anne eagerly read the words illustrating each letter. He mouthed in sequence the sounds of the alphabet, traced each one with his fingers and waited for her to read to him again.

At school, Miss Schmidt gave her attention to children in a specific grade. David had a hard time assimilating all the new things happening and he became a little sleepy. He must have dozed away for a minute when he heard jarring sounds. Children were putting away their books, pens and pencils. It was a frightening clatter and everyone left the classroom for the cloakroom and picked up their lunch kits. All ate and chattered away.

David also got his kit, at first a Rogers Syrup pail. In it was a sandwich, a small jar with milk, and an apple. Later Anne purchased a black lunch kit with space for a regular thermos bottle. David ate in silence watching the others. When lunch time was over, Miss Schmidt declared that it was recess time, whatever that meant, and everyone went outside. Pupils ran around, chased one another; the older ones took a bat and ball and started playing. David watched in admiration.

He walked home accompanied by fellow pupils, but his home was a little further on. They were very friendly and made sure that he continued.

Miss Schmidt was a reassuring and comforting presence. David's mother soon sent a note to her, for the autumn days were getting cooler. As Miss Schmidt followed the note's directions, she ensured that his coat was buttoned and zipped up for his three-and-a-half mile trip home. He walked the round-trip journey by foot each day for the duration of a month and then his father purchased from a fellow farmer a caboose, harness, horse and cart which David then drove to school. He was used to horses on the farm but had not been independent before. Fortunately, the horse was old and slow; it died the following year.

PUPILS SAY DARNDEST THINGS

"Pupils said the darndest things," Miss Schmidt remembered. "On the last day of the school year I received a lovely vase as a gift. The little fellow who gave it to me, warned me, 'Be careful and don't break it. We paid a lot for it.'

"I sent a note along with each pupil indicating that there would be no school the next Tuesday. One pupil did not pass the note to his parents. On what he considered the proper day, he went to school. There was no one there. He did not know what that meant. Did the school disappear? He came home early and told his parents that there was no one there although the school house was still standing.

"One youngster went to the washroom, but came back very quickly in a disturbed condition. 'I can't find it,' he said in tears. "I sent an older boy with him and they returned satisfied. 'Oh, he found it; he just had his underwear on backwards.'"

A child complained to his parents that he had a toothache and so could not go to school. His Dad took him to the dentist who pulled the tooth. Subsequently the parent learned that really there was no toothache, but only a desire not to go to school!

"I was sitting at my desk surrounded by a few children and helping them with math," Miss Schmidt recalled. "The rest of the class worked at their desks. Suddenly I felt something touch my head. I reached up to discover a paper airplane resting on my hair. As I looked up to find the guilty one, the culprit popped up from under his desk with a sheepish grin on his face, as if waiting for me to be angry. I felt like cancelling the recess period, but I just had a laugh, and so did the rest of the class. Then we all settled down to work again."

Male pupils could be quite creative in their pranks on an unsuspecting teacher. Fair game was putting a mouse or garter snake in her desk drawer for company. Other insertions included a pig's or gopher's tail or a giant grasshopper. A few affixed a piece of paper on her with words such as Kick me or some enticing words. Miss Schmidt was mystified by the snickering. She resorted to good detective work or hoped there would be a tattler. Often it was a girl who told.

A note from a parent to the teacher: On Wednesday, David did not come to school because he had to take the cow to the bull. Also, we didn't send him to school on Friday because we thought it was Saturday.

Miss Schmidt had a hard time keeping the multiple grades busy in this one-room rural school. "I'm finished" was a quick reply of one grade. But they could listen to the presentations to the other classes and begin to understand what was pointed out earlier. There was a tendency to fool around. "You have a hard time with the two of us," David related to his mother. "Imagine the job of our teacher taking care of 25!"

"My pupils kept saying the darndest things," Miss Schmidt recalled. "These were often centred on their farm experiences. When the school children heard that horses were shipped and slaughtered as food for minks, they had fun with the idea." Dennis remarked, "It's okay for humans to eat horsemeat, but you just have to pace yourself."

"I think it's all right to eat horsemeat, but one could get the trots," Gilbert chimed in.

"But on the other hand, that could be a stable diet," Marlene noted.

"Enough already," Thelma cautioned, "it's time to say neigh."

This nonsense was delightful. Dennis brought up a problem: how do you define the so-called word, ffffffffffff. He and David sought an answer and found the following: 1. blowing on hot soup, 2. flatulence (fart), and 3. air running out of a tire. "We are really making progress in our education," they concluded. They found words of wisdom in another book:

A thing done right today means no trouble tomorrow.

Words spoken, like eggs broken, are hard to repair.

What you are to be, you are now becoming.

Nobody stumbled into anything sitting down.

Even a fish wouldn't get hooked if he kept his mouth shut.

The only way to have a friend is to be one.

GETTING WATER

Drinking facilities in school were inadequate or non-existent. Often parents sent water in cream cans. But this school did have a well. David was paired with an older student, Raymond, to fetch water. They took a galvanized tin pail along; the well had not been used all summer and Raymond started pumping. The water coming out of the spout was smelly and yellow. And then parts of a gopher emerged.

The two pupils ran back to Miss Schmidt and told her about their experience. She instructed them to keep on pumping until the water got better. They took turns pumping and after a while the water was cold and clear. They cupped their hands and drank and proudly carried a pailful into the school and poured it into a porcelain crock with a push button tap at the bottom. Pupils sometimes used the same cup nearby. An enamel bowl and common towel provided simple washing facilities.

While the pump generally gushed water, after repeated efforts it sometimes refused to spout water. Then pupils had to prime it, for water begat water. But what to do if there was no water at hand? Sometimes they used the water pail to procure some from a nearby slough. But what if the slough had dried up? A few enterprising boys got together and gathered their urine in the pail and used that for priming. It worked although the water was smelly at first.

One day in winter when Raymond and David went for water, a grade seven girl made a snowball from the slushy snow and put it in David's neck and down his back. He shivered and let out a cry and pranced around trying to get rid of the icy mass. Raymond grabbed some snow and made a snow ball and threw it at the aggressor hitting her on the bum. Others came along and everyone had quite a snow fight.

Miss Schmidt had taught at this school the year before. She collected books for a library and tried to persuade the School Unit Office to furnish some rudimentary sports equipment like a soccer ball, softball and bats.

With only one year of teacher training in the Normal School in Saskatoon, Miss Schmidt was a committed young presence in the one-room school. Bachelors in the district soon noticed her. Families knew that one sure way for a young woman to get married on the Prairies was to become a school teacher. Ted was one such farmer who dropped in after school to give her a lift home. Many such teachers found farming to their liking. They settled in the district and became loved and respected members of the community.

Miss Schmidt considered the children's lunches to be quite boring, so she brought from her boarding place some meat stew and cherry crystals for a drink. Little did she know that in doing something special she was challenging the menus of mothers who had often carefully prepared their own individual lunches. When the community became aware of the infusion of additional food and drink, some parents were affronted and approached the pastor and the parent board. The teacher quickly stopped the practice.

The school year was a tense time for Miss Schmidt and her pupils. She sensed that a few of the older boys really did not want to be in the classroom. Their parents had insisted they attend to obtain an education and pupils had to conform because school rules indicated that they remain in school until the age of 15.

During recess time, one of the pupils, Ben, summoned his courage and spoke to Miss Schmidt about his real desire to remain at home and relish the harvesting time, or work for the neighbours and earn some quick cash. He said he was promised $4 a month and a dollar a day during threshing time. Here was a button-nosed 14-year-old arguing his future with a slightly older woman.

During the flag-raising ceremony that very morning, Miss Schmidt noticed all the pupils showed a great interest in the process. During her talk with Ben, she had a brain wave.

"If I let you be the flag-raiser, would you stay in school?" she inquired of Ben.

Miss Schmidt knew that by naming Ben to this position, he would be the number-one boy in school. Ben agreed to be the flag raiser.

"I tell you what, Ben, that flag is frayed on the edges. I will buy a new one, and also some white paint and a brush. You get the older boys to help you paint that pole."

Every morning as pupils lined up, Ben or his assistant raised the flag and Miss Schmidt blew on her little pitch pipe and everyone sang God Save the King. And Miss Schmidt succeeded in keeping Ben at the books.

Miss Schmidt was tiny, red-headed and pretty. And she got pregnant. Who had done it, everyone wondered? It was an awful scandal. She told the head trustee of her predicament. She was getting bigger and bigger but continued teaching in front of the blackboard. The school inspector paid a special visit to the school, but no immediate action was taken.

"Somebody could have charged admission," Barney, a parent, commented. "This has never happened before. 'Don't laugh and poke fun,' my Missus told me."

In the local store, everybody talked about the fact that Miss Schmidt was in a family way, but no one had an easy solution.

One parent suggested that a teacher in the community, Miss Hauser, take over. But she had six children in nine years and already had her hands full.

The Department of Education refused to send a substitute. Miss Schmidt continued to carry on as usual prompting a few suppressed snickers from her pupils. But she indicated that since she was such a growing size and could easily lose her balance, she would not put on a Christmas concert that year and therefore would not have to stand before the community.

"I wonder who was the N in the woodpile," David said. The likely suspect was Elmer, now 16 and only in Grade 5. He stayed in school on Friday evenings to give the floor a thorough sweep, take out the trash and make sure that there was enough wood and coal in the furnace room. He received only a dollar a month, but he was indeed a fast worker, maybe too fast, for he had started at the end of August and this was mid-December and Miss Schmidt was pregnant!

Elmer owned up to what he had done. School times were now a little awkward for both of them. The big lad with his shock of hair and Miss Schmidt had a "shotgun" wedding before the time of delivery. A nice, little wedding. Miss Schmidt had her baby boy all right near the end of the school year.

Parents and other community members were torn between sympathy for the poor couple and a judgment that this was not the right way of doing things. Some said he was very poor—"He didn't have two nickels to rub together." All three of them left the community to work in Alberta. Reports came back that they had more children and became successful farmers.

OUTHOUSES

Grandpa Istvan told David that early farm pioneers had very primitive bathroom facilities. Initially, they placed two poles near a hole in the ground and hung a large cloth or blanket on them to obscure its view, or built an apparatus discreetly screened by bushes. Women, however, soon insisted on an enclosed outhouse, generally a one story two holer. Some had three seats, with ultra modern ones painted inside and out, and insulated with layers of newspaper pasted to the walls; some had real wallpaper. Some had linoleum on the floor and a window up high. Sometimes a vase with crepe-paper flowers sat in the curtained window, an aesthetic feature mostly in female commodes.

These early outhouses were furnished with an outdated Eaton's catalogue that provided material for wiping but also as reading material. Some households used the *Winnipeg Free Press* and *The Western Producer* rather than the catalogue, for their paper was softer. When it was too cold outside, family members used chamber pots conveniently stored under beds; if these were not frozen over night, they were emptied into the outside toilet; otherwise, the ingredients had to be thawed out first. Instead of using the enclosed toilet, however, boys and men often peed behind the house and females also nervously squatted there.

Early school toiletry followed the developing process from the homesteads. St. John's school was no exception. Initially, the toilet was screened by bushes or trees, for pupils wanted to remain anonymous about going into these contraptions. In an effort to keep themselves secure in the later outhouses, some accidently locked themselves in. They then hollered a lot and had to wait for a rescue. Going to this biffy in the winter was an ordeal and time spent therein was understandably quite short. One pupil used an ingenious portable toilet seat which was dry and could be set over the ice laden hole. When not in use, it was hidden in the cloak room and was available to only a privileged few.

At first, rolled toilet paper was provided in this school sanitation fixture, but a gopher took hold of the end of one roll and pulled it all the way to his hole. Rolls seemed to disappear quickly in other ways, for there were many creative uses for them. Since the rolls were expensive, old Eaton's catalogues and outdated newspapers and magazines and even soft grass or broad leaves continued to remain standard fare.

Users of these outside biffies, however, could procure a luxury item. The special treat of Japanese oranges at Christmas came wrapped in soft tissue paper. Those who had this paper could use it instead of the hard variety. At home, pupils often gathered a small supply of these scarce items and hid them. They could be peddled for a small monetary amount, traded for candy, or swapped for the jobs of carrying water to the pigs or gathering eggs.

After pupils moved to a new, modern school, they were treated to a Waterman Waterbury furnace and indoor toilets, one for girls and one for boys, now indispensable conveniences. Waste was deposited into a holding tank, to be pumped out at the end of the school year. Here the luxury item of toilet tissue was necessary for the proper functioning of the chemical septic tank.

At every school board meeting, trustees discussed one notable great expense item—toilet paper. "Had this craze for the modern gone too fast and too far?" trustees questioned. Discussions focused on trying to reduce the wanton paper waste since there was no alternative but this stuff for this modern toilet. Relying on their children's stories, trustees noted the many uses for this handy paper besides the traditional one: to clean pen nibs, as a handkerchief or a towel, to bandage cut fingers, to bundle coins, and to mark the bases on the ball diamond. Trustees were aghast at these creative uses. In conclusion, trustees decided to send a note to Miss Schmidt to make her aware of the great cost and to try and check its unwarranted use.

Smells in school varied, some welcome, others not so much. Some were ordinary: unwashed bodies, manure on boots and pants, wet clothes, cheap perfume, varnish and paint, apples, and meat sandwiches. Others were new for David: oily Dustbane sweeping compound and chalk powder.

DELIGHTED WITH READING

School work centred around the process of reading, whether it was silent reading, oral reading while mouthing the words, literature, memorization, the story hour, topics for composition, or even exercises for grammar. David was so enthralled with the reading process that he again asked Miss Schmidt whether he could take a specific book, *Gulliver's Travels,* a rather advanced book, home. But he was concerned that he might lose it, soil it, or let it get wet from the rain. She agreed, advising him again to take good care of it.

David raced home with it and, sure enough, at the kitchen table, trying to understand the story, he accidentally overturned a cup of water onto it. Anne came to the rescue immediately, mopped up the water with a dish towel, opened the pages, soaked the moisture from them, let them dry and then ironed out the bumps and dimples. She wrote a note to Miss Schmidt, explained what had happened, expressed her sorrow, hoped for leniency and indicated that David would be more careful in the future. Miss Schmidt was very understanding.

This school received from the School Board only a few new reading books each year to replace the dog-eared ones. David enjoyed the Dick and Jane series and moved quickly through the three pre-primer books.

These books depicted a world different from farm life. The emphasis was on living in the city, having fun, dressing in clean and proper clothes, and raising pets at home. This world was unlike the one he experienced where the norm was chores in the morning and evening, often wearing old and worn clothes and playing with animals in the farmyard and in the barn.

In later grades, David welcomed the more difficult readers where he had to go to the common dictionary to find the meaning of words. Line drawings and photos helped illustrate many stories. He liked a drawing of the Red River voyageur, a photo of King George VI in an admiral's uniform, and portraits of Lord Byron and Thomas Hardy.

Reading expanded his Canadian world to include the heroism of Laura Secord, the explorations of Jacques Cartier, Alexander Mackenzie on the Pacific, the Good Doctor of Labrador, Sir Alexander Fleming, Florence Nightingale, Aladdin and his Wonderful Lamp, Pauline Johnson's Lullaby of the Iroquois, and The Sower from the Bible. Grandfather and Grandmother told him about the paintings by Jean Francois Millet which they had seen on their journey from Cherbourg to Canada.

One topic that David's class studied was the Vikings. He found it intriguing that they were descendants of people who had lived in Scandinavia for 10,000 years, and were the ancestors of most of the people who live in Scandinavia today. At the beginning of the Viking Age, Scandinavia included Denmark, Norway, and Sweden. Vikings also gained a toehold in North America.

Many people call all Scandinavians of the earlier period Vikings. They would not call themselves this name today. More accurately Vikings are called Norse although many regarded them as pirates. Interesting was an excavation of a Norse burial site in Norway, including a ship with men buried beside their weapons. There were 15 horses (also four dogs and an oxen), four sleighs, a wagon, farm tools, dishes and buckets, kitchen tools, knives, axes, tethering pegs and dog chains, wheat, apples, luxury foods like walnuts and hazel nuts, beds, quilts, pillows, blankets, three oak chests and clothes, a tapestry and weaving tools. Small tools such as needles, scissors, and knives were attached to the clothing. One woman wore a fine red woolen dress and a white linen veil in a gauze weave, while the another wore a plain blue one with a woolen veil.

The Norse spread over Scotland, England, Ireland, and the Shetland Islands and then Iceland and Greenland. This left them with a short step to North America. Wherever they went they changed the architecture, language, and customs. While in Iceland, the Norse learned that there was still more land to the west. When Leif Eriksson sailed off course in about the year 1,000, he landed in what is now Nova Scotia which he called Vinland. According to 13th and 14th century Icelandic accounts of his life and that of others who would follow, Eriksson was certainly a member of an early Norse voyage to North America, if not in fact the leader of that first expedition.

Other books challenged David to identify great cities, and provided a map of the world, in addition to the rolled one over the blackboard showing in red the vast British Empire. Fascinating were accounts of explorers on camel backs and full-page photos of paintings of Leif Eriksson and Christopher Columbus. These were much more interesting than his earlier readers.

To expand the resources of the school's modest library, the local school unit loaned a wooden box of books to be used for a limited period of time. It was a travelling library. In addition, some pupils, like David and Theresa, subscribed to the Saskatchewan Information Library in Regina for more books. They indicated which books in the catalogue they wanted; these books would arrive free of charge and were to be returned by a specified date, postage free.

David took one of these books to school, *Ali Baba and the 40 Thieves*, and placed it in his desk. Miss Schmidt noticed it and asked David whether she could use it to read to the entire class right after recess time. He readily agreed.

For David, reading was always a delight. Louie and Anne ensured that he knew the English language and the alphabet before going to grade school, for early on only Hungarian was spoken at home. Louie recalled his unhappy experience in grade one. The classes in the morning were in German and in English during the afternoon. Unfortunately, he did not know either of these languages and began to cry. Now he vowed that his children, although they spoke only Hungarian at home, would learn English before they began school. Anne began to teach David the alphabet and, in the winter, she interrupted the lessons to help Louie outdoors. He went with an open sleigh to gather logs to be used to provide winter heat; with each load, Anne went outside to help him unload, lifting the lighter ends.

She then went into the warm house and read to David *Lullaby of the Iroquois* by Pauline Johnson. The simple, lilting and earthy words fascinated him. He reflected on the poem's meaning and slowly, mentally but also softly mouthed the words:

> Little brown baby-bird, lapped in your nest,
> Wrapped in your nest,
> Strapped in your nest,
> Your straight little cradle-board rocks you to rest;
> Its hands are your nest;
> Its bands are your nest;
> It swings from the down-bending branch of the oak;
> You watch the camp flame, and the curling grey smoke;
> But, oh, for your pretty black eyes sleep is best—
> Little brown baby of mine, go to rest.

David was so enthralled with the poem that he again asked Miss Schmidt whether he could take this reader home. He pointed out to his mother that there was another poem by the same author that could serve as a soft song and bedtime story. "I read *The Song My Paddle Sings* in school and although I have never gone canoeing, the poem has a great rhyme. I know Pauline Johnson is writing about my country and her Indian country."

Proudly, he read parts of it to his mother, knowing that thereby he was practicing and mastering his reading skills.

> West wind, blow from your prairie nest,
> Blow from the mountains, blow from the west.
> The sail is idle, the sailor too;
> O wind of the west, we wait for you!
> Blow, blow!

"I enjoy the pictures of dangers that she paints," David reflected.

> Dash, dash,
> With a mighty crash,
> They seethe and boil and bound and splash.
> Be strong, O paddle! be brave, canoe!
> The reckless waves you must plunge into.

"I like her repetition and imitating sounds for Johnson's style gives the poem a feeling of saying-it-while-walking-along. I like to read it aloud when no one can hear me. She has become my friend.

"The notes in this book state that actually Pauline Johnson was a Mohawk Indian from Ontario. When she wrote this poem, she wore Native clothing. She also enjoyed reading tales about Native peoples, such as Longfellow's epic poem, *The Song of Hiawatha*. I will have to read that also."

Another poem David relished was *Little Bateese* by William Henry Drummond, for this young boy was much like himself; he started to memorize parts of it. He appreciated Leetle Bateese's playfulness, his mischievous behaviour, although some of it was really dumb. It was so nice to be a kid in this funny, broken language, mixing English and French. David could enter a Quebec farmer's world with its chickens, cows, cranes and canoes. It was so much like his own.

"I laughed with the poetry," he recounted.

You bad leetle boy, not moche you car How busy you're kipin' your poor gran'per Tryin' to stop you ev'ry da Chasin' de hen aroun' de ha W'y don't you geev' dem a chance to lay? Leetle Bateese!

Off on de fiel' you foller de ploug Den w'en you're tire you scare de co Sickin' de dog till dey jomp de wal So de milk ain't good for not'ing at al An' you're only five an' a half dis fall, Leetle Bateese!

"I also wonder what my parents and grandparents really think of the stupid things I often do," David thought.

In the poem, grandfather realizes and accepts his own mortality as he gazes at Bateese sleeping, for he will never live to see his grandson carry a canoe on that long portage. With pride he imagines the strength, maybe like the strongest man ever, Louis Cyr, and the ability this remarkable little boy will have as he grows to manhood.

David was especially fascinated with the last stanza where grandfather loves his grandson despite all his foibles and wants him to remain that way forever. He imagined, or at least hoped, that this might have been the case with his own grandparents.

But leetle Bateese! please don't forge We rader you're stayin' de small boy yet So chase de chicken an' mak' dem scar An' do w'at you lak wit' your ole gran'per For w'en you're beeg feller he won't be dere, Leetle Bateese!

The next poem David read was *The Vision of Sir Launfal* by James Russell Lowell. Here the story, unlike that of Leetle Bateese, was foreign to David's world. His grade had the task of memorizing parts of it and then reciting it in front of the teacher. Each of the pupils took the reader outside and went behind the horse barn or among the caragana bushes to be alone and commit it to memory. David sat on the ground near his cart and read the words aloud. He chewed them and breathed them in. Even though the images were strange, he explored them and ventured in.

Miss Schmidt had explained the gist of the poem and David memorized parts of it with that in mind. In the poem, an Arthurian knight searches for the Holy Grail, the cup Jesus used at the Last Supper with his apostles. David could identify with the beauty of nature in this lengthy poem, but a lot of the ideas were over his head. Joseph of Arimathea brought this cup to England and people made pilgrimages to it. The one who kept it had to be holy and pure. One of the keepers lost his purity and then the cup disappeared.

Hard to understand were words such as "Each ounce of dross costs its ounce of gold; For a cap and bells our lives we pay, Bubbles we earn with a whole soul's tasking."

Miss Schmidt explained that another poet, William Wadsworth Longfellow, gathered material for *The Song of Hiawatha* from many Ojibwe people. He wanted to form a lasting story and he began with the spirit, Gitche Manito, who brings the various tribes together to smoke the peace pipe. This Great Spirit also sends a prophet to the people, Hiawatha; he lives with his grandmother, Nokomis, who teaches him about nature.

In the fourth section of the poem, Hiawatha goes to see his father, the West Wind, which praises him and defines his mission in life: Go back to your home and people; live and work among them, cleanse the earth from all that harms it; clear the fishing grounds and rivers, slay all monsters and magicians.

> By the shores of Gitche Gumee,
> By the shining Big-Sea-Water,
> Stood the wigwam of Nokomis,
> Daughter of the Moon, Nokomis.
> Dark behind it rose the forest,
> Rose the black and gloomy pine-trees,
> Rose the firs with cones upon them;
> Bright before it beat the water,
> Beat the clear and sunny water,
> Beat the shining Big-Sea-Water.

"I liked reading parts of this poem aloud to catch its rhythm, much like a bedtime song to lull me to sleep. Longfellow mixes human beings and nature and I began to dream about things with him. The poem is so nice but I heard sad things about the Indians also," David reflected.

PENMANSHIP

The printed letters of the alphabet were prominent on the upper part of the school blackboard. Pupils learned to copy them more or less exactly and then put them together to form words. The greater challenge was to loop these letters in long hand, a task of penmanship. It required hand to eye coordination, finger and hand movements, repetitive drills, but it was faster than printing.

At school, Miss Schmidt had daily exercises in penmanship in all grades. She wrote on the blackboard in cursive script, samples pupils could imitate.

"Use straight strokes and work in clockwise, counter-clockwise and combined circles," she suggested. "Don't slump over at your desk. Check how you are doing by comparing your writing with the examples. Get into a rhythm. After a while you will be so sure of yourselves that you won't even think about it for it will come naturally."

Positioning the body was important as well as shoulder and arm movements. She showed pupils how to strengthen their arm and finger muscles to ensure beautiful writing.

Miss Schmidt did not attempt to change left-handers to right ones, as some teachers did.

She instructed pupils on how to use straight pens with detachable nibs. The pens were scratchy and prone to blotting but the biggest problem was the pesky ink. It was difficult to pour from a quart-size ink container into smaller inkwells recessed in their desks without dripping and spilling. The older students were entrusted with this task but even then there were splatters of the permanent ink. Rags and blotting papers were then needed.

At times pupils worked on a large table and used a small bottle of ink. They did lots of painstaking work in tablets, on a map, posters, drawings, only to have everything ruined when someone upset the bottle. Often their clothes were covered with ink, the table and floor forming a blue tide. It happened so fast. They quickly looked for blotters. Miss Schmidt stopped teaching, got a washbasin, rags, and gave the clothing a good rinsing. On their hands and knees, pupils helped her mop the floor. There was no scolding for who knows who might be the next one causing an accident.

But there were some jokers, mostly older boys who messed with the pigtails of the girl in the desk in front of them. Yielding to temptation, they dipped the ends of pigtails into a convenient inkwell behind a female pupil. Sometimes they made squiggly designs on paper with the tails. Miss

Schmidt meted out harsh punishment to the perpetrators; also, these pranksters made spitballs soaked with ink. To stem this foolishness, Miss Schmidt quickly came up with an alternative seating arrangement: boys would sit in the front of the rows with girls in the back; no more temptations to fool with pigtails!

Marlene recalled a most embarrassing and funny moment during recess. A mildly aggressive boy, Billy, kissed her and she squealed on him to the teacher in front of all her classmates. A split second later, Billy opened the door and ran all the way home. What humiliation! He didn't show up at school for the next two weeks. He thought the teacher would strap him but she carried on as usual.

While early on, pupils used pens with nibs for writing, some pupils from more wealthy families used fountain pens and after a while ballpoint ones. Louie proudly told David that a Hungarian, Laszlo Biro, had invented a modern ballpoint pen. It was introduced into Canada eventually, and Louie purchased one of the first in the district, a quite expensive Reynolds Rocket for your Pocket.

Made of aluminum with a retractable end to protect the ball, it was advertised as being able to write under water and would last for 15 years without refilling. However, it gave smudged results and soon ran out of ink. Since refills were not made for the Reynolds pen, Louie bought one of another brand, inserted it into a wooden holder and placed it in the original pen. He reluctantly loaned it to David to use in school; David proudly displayed it by clipping it to his shirt pocket.

The Anne and Louie household made the most of every piece of paper; they got into the habit of saving blank sheets no matter where they came from—calendar pages, pieces of cardboard, brown wrapping paper, paper bags and used envelopes. Many of these items were handy for composing shopping lists and notes.

David remembered one of the first topics he had to write on when he returned to school in the fall. It was How I spent my summer holidays, a rather strange topic for a farm boy; perhaps Miss Schmidt was following some school directive in giving this assignment to these rural pupils. David thought it might have been retitled, How I EXPECTED to spend my summer holidays, for rural students rarely had holidays in the summer and fall. Instead, they stayed at home and worked harder than ever.

He recalled, however, that the whole family did go to the Saskatoon Fair and took lunch along. After morning chores were done, they drove to the city. He and his Dad spent all of their time inspecting new farm machinery and its prices while Theresa and Mom examined the craft and bakery displays. They noticed a ferris wheel and other rides on the fairgrounds, but did not partake in them for they took at least a half an hour and cost money. They returned home in time for the evening chores.

In his school exercise, David recalled this non-thrilling event in a few sentences, then extended it and embellished it with exciting rides and activities. Over all, quite an imaginary summer holiday.

Miss Schmidt engaged pupils in several challenging exercises. In one, she spoke 10 words that pupils had to write correctly. If needed, they could check the common dictionary for accuracy. They had to have a clean handkerchief, learn proper etiquette and politeness.

The recess break began with pupils going to the cloak room and bringing their lunch kits to their desks. They sometimes found surprises in lunch boxes such as a chicken leg, a piece of saskatoon/june berry pie and even store-bought cookies; boiled eggs could be cracked on unsuspecting foreheads.

It was a time for kidding around and chattering. Then most pupils hurried to the playground. Summer and fall were ideal times to play softball and in winter both boys and girls played foot hockey. In the absence of pucks, horse apples had to do; it was great fun until a pupil was hit in the mouth. Later, when Louie procured a soccer ball from the School Unit, they played soccer on packed snow with stumps or felt boots as goal posts.

When the snow drifted to form high banks, it was fun to dig holes into them and make interconnecting tunnels. Angeline fell into one of them and broke her wrist. Since the snow banks were so towering, pupils carried the school water pail up the high drifts and placed it on top of the flag pole just as repairmen for the telegraph lines put their lunch pails on top of their poles. Some attempted to be the king of the snow castles until they were pummeled with snow balls in an effort to make them come down from their perches. When it rained, pupils played tag, cops and robbers or soccer in the basement.

During recess time, Miss Schmidt again noticed in David's desk a story book which was not part of the school's library; it was from the Saskatchewan Information Library. After the allotted time for recess, Miss Schmidt rang a bell summoning pupils and then asked David whether she could use this specific book for afternoon readings. He readily agreed to the reading of *Dr. Doolittle*. Even though these stories were engaging for him, several pupils rested their heads on their desks and had a short snooze.

Dr. John Dolittle was the central character of a series of children's books by Hugh Lofting starting in 1920 with *The Story of Doctor Dolittle*. He was a doctor who shunned human patients in favour of animals with whom he spoke in their own languages. He later became a naturalist, using his abilities to speak with animals to better understand nature and the history of the world.

Lofting began to write these stories when he was a soldier in the trenches during World War I. Since he found the war either too horrible or dull, he wrote illustrated letters to children. In these creations, Dr. Dolittle lives in the fictional village of Puddleby-on-the-Marsh in the West Country. He has a few close human friends, including Tommy Stubbins and Meinrad Mugg, the Cats'-Meat Man.

Pupils generally found these imaginative stories enchanting for they were not far removed from their own farm lives and seemed addressed to them alone. Lofting penned in a child-like way as in the beginning of the book: "He [Dr. Dolittle] was very fond of animals and kept many kinds of pets. Besides the gold-fish in the pond at the bottom of his garden, he had rabbits in the pantry, white mice in his piano, a squirrel in the linen closet and a hedgehog in the cellar. He had a cow with a calf too, and an old lame horse—twenty-five years of age—and chickens, and pigeons, and two lambs, and many other animals. But his favorite pets were Dab-Dab the duck, Jip the dog, Gub-Gub the baby pig, Polynesia the parrot, and the owl Too-Too."

INEXPENSIVE SCRIBBLERS

For school work, David's parents bought him several inexpensive scribblers or tablets which had an attractive picture on the front while the back was covered with mathematical tables up to 12 times 12, pictures of birds, other animals, children at play, and breathtaking scenes of all parts of Canada. He used a scribbler for each subject.

He also had a pencil box, a narrow wooden container with a sliding lid where he could safely store pencils, pens, pen nibs, and erasers. Some pupils could not afford a store-bought pencil box and used a cigar box or a cardboard chocolate one instead. These would be handy and larger, especially for boys, to house grasshoppers, spiders, gopher tails, baby mice or bird eggs.

In the evening Miss Schmidt wrote exam questions on the blackboard and put the large map over them to shield them from prying eyes. Some words appeared over the map's edges and piqued creative minds.

Guidelines for the school construction indicated that the classroom window area should be one-fifth of the floor area. Windows opened west to a grassy area and lots of caragana bushes. Not too much distraction except for some occasional birds and an old Titan tractor chugging along.

As David viewed the blackboard atlas and the Pool elevator's Saskatchewan map, he was enamored with place names. He played a game with himself: say the names quietly, Osoyoos, Saskatoon, Saskatchewan, Moose Jaw; a variant to saying them inauspiciously was to give throat to the German names, to Austrian towns: Muenster, St. Gregor, Bremen, Fulda; or, bray the cloud names: stratus, nimbus stratus, cumulus, cirrus; mouth the names of relatives he knew: Julie, Hansie, Tony, Girlie, Mary, Annie, Frankie, Boysie, and Eddie. Saying the words softly was soothing; hearing them mentally was stimulating.

When the weather was stormy in the winter and pupils did not venture out during recess, Miss Schmidt invented work for them to do at their desks; samples were: take a page from your reading lesson and arrange the words in alphabetical order; make a list of all the words from your reading pages containing a given sound, for example, take the K sound (corn, car, king, cracker).

From a list of words on the blackboard, write the word and then its opposite, for example, up, then, down. Write the names of creatures that fly, that run, jump, swim, or creep. Write the names of animals that growl, purr, cackle, sing, laugh, neigh, bark. This playful exercise stirred imaginations and increased vocabulary, particularly if pupils had to look them up in the dictionary to learn their meanings and spellings.

Miss Schmidt threw out another challenge to her pupils; she would record the names of the first one to notice the signs of the coming of spring, the first to spot a flock of geese, the first to spy a crow, a meadowlark, robin, grasshopper, gopher, crocus, blade of grass. Pupils would police themselves for the truth of these sightings for their names and the objects would be written on the blackboard.

Marlene enthusiastically spoke of hearing a meadowlark sprinkling its song with varied melodies; Allan noted that a hawk swung overhead like an anchor; Angeline recalled the sky wearing a necklace of wild geese. Others were keen observers of nature in general: the flaming beauty of a prairie sunset, a late winter morning whiskered with hoar frost, water chuckling down a hillside, summer rusting into autumn.

Rural life also had its irritants and predominant among them were mosquitoes. Some infested the classroom and were squished in tablet pages. Before passing a slough of water, pupils took a deep breath and then ran by as fast as we could. Even then, mosquitoes rose like a big black cloud and swarmed after them. The air was so thick that breathing drew them into their nostrils.

Some pupils engaged in a game: each permitted a mosquito to settle on an arm or leg and watched it gorge itself on blood. When it was well-bloated, they crushed it. Its blood dried on the skin. The competition was to see who had the biggest splotch of dried blood. Some individuals seemed immune to mosquito bites, or at least after these bites they had no swelling or itching.

Even though houses had screens on windows and doors, flies managed to get indoors. Although they did not bite, they were dirty and a pesky nuisance especially in the fall. They danced in the air, drowned in the drinking water and caressed and tickled faces with their tufted feet. David had to fend them from food, kill them with a fly swatter and catch them with coiled, sticky flypaper. Spraying them with the chemical DDT was common. There was an endless number of flies for they loved manure, the outhouse and sweets. No wonder there were songs such as Shoo fly, don't bother me, and I know an old lady who swallowed a fly.

RESCUING BLACK BABIES

Miss Schmidt invited the pastor of St. John's, Father Bernard, to school.

"I am delighted to be with you now and not only in my catechism classes," he said. He knew that he was among children from Roman Catholic families and so he advised them and their parents to become foreign missionaries. He pointed to many countries in Africa and Asia which he called uncivilized; there was a lot of poverty and many abandoned pagan children. He said he was a member of the Association of the Holy Childhood which rescues children whose parents have deserted them and left them to die because they did not have enough food.

Father Bernard appealed to the pupils' sense of heroism in this rescue. "All of you can become missionaries to help these desperate children and to baptize them," he said. "You can't actually go to Africa which is far away, but you can rescue bodies and souls from hardship. You and your parents can become missionaries by your prayers and offerings. You can give a little money for there are 18 million babies who have already been saved and baptized, even though most of them did not long survive their baptism."

He handed Miss Schmidt and her pupils attractive cards with a picture of a ransomed baby and an invitation to buy a black baby for a dollar. Those who contributed could select the baptismal name of the child. "This is a black baby crusade to buy little godchildren from the slavery of the devil and help them appear before the throne of God," Father Bernard concluded.

PLAYING GAMES

In winter, some children came to school in an open sleigh box. At recess time, the older girls sat in that box and talked about their hair and clothes. To pull a prank, the older boys started to tip that box and eventually upset it, forcing the girls to exit screaming.

This school was tucked into a wooded area, with bush on its three sides. During summer at noon and recess times, pupils enjoyed playing in the cool of the school grove of caragana trees. As they tramped out make-shift rooms, they played their favorite game of store, fashioning items and selling them. In imitation of parents and storekeepers, they carried on a thriving business, using empty cartons and cans to create display tables, a register with a cash drawer, and a bell indicating sales. Miss Schmidt encouraged this business-like approach for pupils were practiced their adding, subtracting and multiplying skills.

David welcomed the demands of arithmetic. One challenge was to calculate the difference between 10.2 and 2.345, add the product of 0.2 and 43.68 and divide the sum by 2.5. Grammar was more puzzling, for instance, a lesson called for the writing of the possessive case, singular and plural, of man, thief, child, heiress.

Parts of speech had their own difficulties, which Miss Schmidt could not always clarify; these centred around nouns, gerunds, gerundives and participles; specifically, in There is a run in one's stocking; is run a verb or a noun? What about the sentences, I ran to the barn and I am running. Yes, they are often action words, but what about To run is great and Running is great?

Pupils took nature hikes in the fall. The treasures they found were the same as on the farm, but there was something special in doing the same thing as a school project. Treasured items were birds' nests, coloured leaves, lichen and moss. The boys found an interesting and puzzling set of objects; they were crocks apparently used for some purpose. They offered guesses about why they were hidden in the woods; a couple of the older boys snickered as they revealed the use of these contraptions: they were for making whisky, called white lightning, and these brewers did not want to be associated with them for fear that police with dogs would find them and throw them in jail.

On one of the last days of June, the older boys were lying on the grass, watching the clouds and guessing what their summer would be like. In a frolicking mood, the older girls picked out specific boys, the good-looking girl for the good-looking boy, and laid down on each one.

During recess, some naughty boys detached the line used to raise the flag and used it as a lariat in a game of cowboys and Indians. Ben and the teacher considered this a lack of respect for the monarch. Miss Schmidt asked the culprits to stay after school and write out many times, I will honor the king.

One of the games the boys liked to play behind the horse barn was to best each other in peeing a long distance and then vie with one another as to how far their ejaculations could spew. They did not realize, or chose not to, that the girls were peeking around the corner and watching. "I could use one of those things; they look really handy," Marlene remarked.

The school and farm environment provided ample time to be a kid. Games at school like tag, prisoners' base, ante ante over, hide and seek, hop-scotch, London bridge, fox and goose and softball were opportunities for both boys and girls of all ages to participate. On the farm, especially when relatives visited on Sundays, riding bikes provided fascinating recreation.

The gathering of the clan represented a hiving of creative possibilities: for boys and sometimes for girls, snaring gophers, skating, riding pigs or calves, sliding down haystacks and climbing trees. David's cousins did more daring things than he was permitted. They liked to visit the straw pig barn, rob the sparrow nests, and taunted and fled from an angry bull.

Children learned many lessons in school and at home: take your turn, lose without whining, win without grandstanding, endure your lumps and bruises and keep on trying, cooperate and stick together, tattling doesn't pay. If you want to skate, you have to shovel the snow off the ice; if you want the thrill of swooping down a hill, you have to climb to the top. Beside individual and group benefits, these interactions also burned calories and honed physical reflexes.

While doing kid things and having fun, rural children missed many opportunities. There was little expert coaching in sports, few dancing or skating lessons. They knew the ways of gophers, coyotes, and badgers but never saw a llama or a lion. They knew the benefits of listening to art and music appreciation classes on the radio, but they never frequented art galleries, attended music concerts or visited libraries.

In the absence of many toys and props for games, children relied on their imagination and determination. The simple games were varied, ranging from team sports such as softball, to tag. Since there were so few pupils in school, everyone had a role to play. Positions were rotated; children learned to take turns.

Pupils learned to do by doing. There was little instruction or coaching on how to do things. They observed one another. From the school grove of caragana trees, they picked bushels of ripe pods for seed to sell to the Indian Head Tree Nursery. Monies realized also went to cover expenses for their Christmas concert. They seldom travelled outside the community and knew of other peoples and countries mostly from adult reports, books and the radio.

"We had time to daydream and do kid things," David recalled. "We knew crocuses in patches of snow, tiger lilies, lady slippers and fireweeds. We saw gophers and coyotes but not elephants and hyenas. We recognized the words opera and symphony but did not know what they meant."

A highlight of the school year was a June field day for district schools held in a nearby town. It was a sort of micro-Olympics. Pupils practiced very little for the event, but, nevertheless, tried varied lengths of the dash, high and broad jump and sack races. The length of a dash was marked by stepping out the distance. Since David's school did not feel that their softball team was good enough, they did not enter that competition with town schools. On the field day Louie came with his open truck box, gathered pupils and drove them there. Miss Schmidt rode with him in the cab.

"It was a great feeling with the wind in our face and hair," David said of the open truck trip. "At the grounds, each of us received a ticket to be punched for individual purchases. We could buy pop and ice cream. At the track, we proudly lined up behind our school banner.

"Very few from our school won any event; those who did, received a ribbon or pennant for first, second or third in the competitions of racing, jumping, softball, broad jump, and high jump. In the afternoon it rained and children took refuge under the truck box. In the evening there was a movie in the local theatre."

While in town with his Dad, and although he had little money, David made a special effort to buy coloured peppermint candies with smart, loving sayings printed on them in red sugar. He wanted to impress Marlene who sat across from him in school and so he passed them to her when the teacher wasn't looking in his direction.

But Marlene never took time to read his candies; instead, she gave him a friendly smile and popped them quickly into her mouth and went on with her schoolwork as if nothing had happened. His cute attempt had vanished, for he was too timid to point out the candy messages. But maybe she knew about these special candies, for although she was from a rather wealthy family according to prairie standards, she was timid herself about a possible relationship.

Going to school was a stimulating experience with opportunities to learn so many new things and to prepare for Christmas concerts which were held at first in the old church. In softball games, the girls challenged the boys. Their steady teasing of can't hit, can't pitch, can't catch had a negative effect on the boys. One of them, the pitcher, had the nickname of muskrat because of his large buck teeth and the girls took full advantage in their taunting. This mild warfare must have worked, for the girls won most of the games.

In the spring and early summer, softball games against neighbouring schools provided several outings. At a school nearby, the dust from the dry fields whirled as the teams competed. The school's teacher, Mr. Brown, was the umpire and his face bore the impact of the dust. We noted how apt it was that his name was Mr. Brown!

Our class formed a team and vied with other teams to be the best spellers in the school. Some words were exceedingly difficult, even the word Saskatchewan. We remembered it through the individual letters in the saying, Sue And Sally Killed Turkey, Chased Him East, West And North. The losing team had to stay after school and wash the floor, pound out the erasers and sweep the floor.

David complained to his father that the school had so few bats, only one softball and no gloves. Louie told him that in his day, they used stout branches from trees as bats and made their own softball. "Once the ball started to unravel, somebody would take it home and get a parent to fix it. No purchased swings, instead, two poles were dug in the ground with a pole across the top and old horse collars tied to a rope served as seats. The collars smelled from horse sweat, but we had fun."

VISITING SUPERINTENDENT

This rural school generally knew the date and time of the superintendent's visitation beforehand.

"We have to tidy up our classroom, the cloak room and the basement for the school inspector is coming first thing in the morning," Miss Schmidt instructed the pupils, "and when he comes, we will all stand and say, 'Good morning, Mr. Germain.'"

And Mr. Germain, the inspector, did come right on time in a black Chevy coupe. Tall, lanky and balding, he noticed that some pupils were playing softball before school time began. He approached one of the older girls and asked whether she was the teacher. Thelma timidly told him that she was not but instead a pupil in the school.

As he entered the school, he observed Miss Schmidt putting class assignments on the blackboard. He was especially interested in music, for he immediately gravitated toward the small battery-operated turntable in a far corner. He picked up a record and examined it carefully before he taught the pupils to breathe properly and then sing a song called Michael Finnegan, an old man who grew whiskers on his chinnigan.

Mr. Germain was interested in everything: the condition of the fence surrounding the school and its yard, the flag and flag pole, the water supply, closets and toilets, the barn, general appearance of grounds, the school records, especially punctuality and regularity of attendance, the general standing and progress of the classes and the attitudes of both teacher and pupils.

He checked the books in the modest library, ambled to the turntable again, and picked up a record. He indicated he was interested in what the pupils knew: Did they know their timetables? Did they know Canada's provinces and their major cities? Could they recite any poetry?

Pupils tried their best to answer his questions correctly, for it they did not, their poor teacher might look like an ambushed deer or a doe head. They felt that they and Miss Schmidt were in this together.

The grade ones came and sat on the teacher's lap to read. The superintendent confessed that he had never seen this before, but he had to acknowledge that they were certainly learning to read. "I think they are trying so hard and doing so well because they want to please you," Miss Schmidt said.

It was noon and Miss Schmidt indicated to the students that they should stand; she then led them in a short prayer before lunch time.

Barbara was in the lineup for prayers, but she could not hold her water any longer. It flushed out and spread to the floor. She was terribly embarrassed and started to cry. Miss Schmidt rushed and picked up a towel and mopped up the mess. Everyone in the class was apprehensive, wondering what a bad impression they were making on the inspector. This had happened before and they hoped it would not happen again, at least not in the presence of the inspector.

But the foreigner did not seem to notice. He continued to loom over the class behind all the desks as the pupils furtively glanced at him. At the beginning of prayers, he did not make the sign of the cross. Was he Catholic as all pupils were? Was he really praying like the rest? He was a mystery man almost from outer space.

After his visit, he filed a report in quadruplicate: one to the trustees, one to the teacher, another to Department of Education and one for himself.

"It was a pleasure to teach in that one-room rural school," Miss Schmidt reflected later on. "I insisted they wear shoes in the classroom, but some of them took them off and played barefoot or walked home that way. Felt boots were warm in winter and some girls donned babushkas just like their mothers.

"I can still see their lively eyes and red cheeks. Every day I could envision their minds opening up like flowers to the sun. Although most of them were of German background, they were no longer coming to school to learn English and take it back to the sod shack or the shanty and teach their parents. Children in the earlier generation had accompanied their father when he took a load of grain or shopped for groceries in town; the parent wanted someone who knew English quite well so that he would appear knowledgeable in the process and not be cheated. After school, these pupils would teach specific words to their parents: they would point to a chair, if they had one, and say chair, and their parents would repeat that word.

"Both children and parents were quick learners for they had a great desire to know their new culture. In my modest way I realized I was bringing a form of civilization to the Prairies. At first, we had only a few old dog-eared books. There were not many writing tablets for most of the work was done on the blackboard. We teachers had a humble attitude about ourselves for we considered ourselves members of the community, serving its needs and we were not really professionals, just teachers, for doctors and lawyers were the only professionals."

CHOCOLATE BAR MAPS

Every school in Canada received a letter from The Copp Clark Company, a printing and publishing firm in Toronto, that it could receive two maps free of charge, one of Canada and another of the world. These maps, rolled on a wooden rod, were supplied by the chocolate company, William Neilson Limited, and came with the stipulation that the advertising of Neilson chocolate bars on the map corners not be obliterated in any way. Updated maps could be replaced upon request.

From these unfurled maps hanging on the top of blackboards, pupils learned their geography while salivating for these bars, purchased rather rarely. Because of this advertising, the maps acquired several nicknames: chocolate-flavored map, sweet map, map that made your mouth water every time you studied from it, map with its oceans filled with candy bars.

These tantalizing bars were: Neilson's Jersey Milk Chocolate, Neilson's Jersey Nut, Neilson's Malted Milk Candy Bar, Neilson's Crispy Crunch, and Neilson's Cocoa.

On a detailed map of Saskatchewan, David noticed that the land was laid out in geometrical patterns like fences on a property. The province was easy to draw but hard to spell.

When these maps were no longer in use, they were rolled up and replaced by class exercises or drawings. A teacher or the school could purchase, or make stencils with a sewing machine—tiny perforations on hard paper which could be placed on a surface, and patted gently with a coloured, chalk-filled brush; varied designs appeared magically to create beautiful effects: patterns of birds, fishes, water life, insects, flowers, plants and trees; people of different nationalities, borders, special designs, and maps.

Miss Schmidt changed the motifs with the seasons: lilies or bunnies at Easter; strutting turkeys at Thanksgiving; pumpkins and witches at Halloween; poppies and crosses on Remembrance Day; the crib, tree, reindeer and Santa Claus at Christmas; daffodils or crocuses during spring. These depictions had to be changed regularly for it was boring and out of place to see those of Christmas during Easter.

There were also stencils for the alphabet, and provincial capitals and lower-case letters to encourage proper penmanship; also, numbers 1 to 10, printed and written. Often the school had no funds for these stencils, so Miss Schmidt bought them with her own money. She enlisted especially the taller pupils to learn from these examples and then add their own images to the top of the blackboard, visible to the whole school.

Raymond, tall and mischievous, clandestinely changed a few details on these pictures. Santa acquired a protrusion between his legs; a bird lost a wing and a woman received a big nose. Much snickering erupted when pupils recognized these changes. At first Miss Schmidt was mystified by these reactions, then she thought them clever and funny, but did not want to draw attention to them or encourage them, so she unobtrusively, at recess, restored the images to their proper form.

LEARNING GAMES

There were various learning games, with older pupils being captains and selecting younger pupils to form their team; every pupil had a chance to play. In one game pupils were challenged to write any geographical place on the blackboard with a point given for each letter in the name. A pupil in the next team had to begin the next word with the last letter of the previous word. Instead of geography, the subjects were also farming and literature. The team that received the highest total score won.

There was a lesson on old Greek history. The topic was the heating of Greek homes during their cold weather. The Greeks had no stoves, furnaces, or fireplaces so they used flaming braziers, pans filled with burning coals, to warm their rooms. As David was writing a summary of this topic, he substituted brassieres for braziers. Then he read his summary to the class. On only one face was there a small smile indicating recognition of his error. He realized his mistake and concluded that flaming brassieres would not heat a Greek room very much!

There was a lot of time between lessons and David took some foolscap paper and started doodling. He liked to draw faces with all kinds of funny features. Sometimes he left these drawings on his desktop and one time the older boys noticed them and put the names of pupils under each one of these weird faces. David hoped the teacher did not notice this.

PRANKS

It was near Halloween time, Friday, the last day of the school week. Everyone in school pitched in to render the floor spic and span; they rearranged the maps and library books, put the desks in perfect rows. What a stunning surprise when on the following Monday morning everything was disheveled. Miss Schmidt was disconcerted and puzzled. She looked as though she wanted to go home.

The library books were littered from one end of the room to the other. Desks were overturned with tablets, rulers, pencil boxes, erasers, crayons, pens and pencils scattered all over. The phono radio was on the floor sitting on its side. Miss Schmidt's desk was emptied of papers. Coal chunks were strewn all over. What a mess!

Miss Schmidt immediately penned a note to Louie to inform him of the disaster. The children, however, showed an eagerness and energy to put things aright. They were not resentful but cooperative, considerate and responsible. The desks were placed upright and in a straight line; they sorted through everything, placed them in appropriate stacks for individual pupils.

Miss Schmidt began to share their enthusiasm as she collected her papers and put the books in alphabetical order. The boys took the lumps of coal to the furnace room. The dust was the hardest to contain for, after sweeping, some still remained. The girls washed the floor. The cleanup took all morning but everyone worked together. No one in the district owned up to wreaking the devastation; no one found out who did it, but the school was now locked after hours.

Halloween in town was a time not only for trick or treating; it was a time to play pranks. Some residents were vigilant for they did not want any destruction to their buildings or machinery. They turned outside lights on at night and kept an eye out through their windows. But incidents happened: outdoor toilets were overturned, filled oil drums were rolled to cover the streets; mischief prevailed.

On one farm, some imps decided to disassemble a buggy and reassemble it on top of a machine shed. It was painstaking task and all went according to plan until the owner got wind of the prank, hid in the bushes, watched the operation and when it was completed, emerged and commanded the pranksters to reverse the operation. It did not work out well. A prank reversed.

Gilbert was called a nixnuts in school. He was 12 years old and his darting blue eyes were always searching for something devilish. He had a plump, smirky face topped by a mop of unruly brown hair and was always ready to find time for extracurricular activities. On one occasion, he filled a girl's hat with slushy snow and then clamped it on her head. He thought it a great joke.

On another occasion he pricked a girl in her arm with a compass. He began to strew a wire across the aisle so as to trip someone. As he was doing so, Miss Schmidt asked him to rewind all the wire on a spool and put it on her desk.

"Young man, make yourself useful by taking over from me and teaching for the rest of the day. Up in front. I will be Gilbert and I'll sit in your desk and do your work." When pupils had questions about grammar, they came to Gilbert. But he could not help them. Some became rowdy in the classroom and he could not control them. Irene asked him to place Timbuktu on a map but he could not find it. His classmates began to dislike and distrust him.

He dismissed the class for recess and wanted to join them, but Miss Schmidt said, "Sorry, you can't leave; too much work to do; prepare the grade one reading lesson, put grade four spelling work on the blackboard, check grade six." Gilbert broke down and cried; he wanted to be restored to plain old Gilbert. In the future, whenever Gilbert started acting up, Miss Schmidt merely pointed to the teacher's chair and Gilbert would turn red and hang his head. He was no more trouble.

In the summer, David and Theresa went to school with a cart and horse. On their return, they often amicably discussed what had happened in school that day, but on this occasion, they had a contentious argument; they batted one another and Theresa's long, beautiful, hand-knitted scarf got caught in the cart's wheel, spun around the axle and sopped up axle grease. Their mother was not too pleased.

Charlie was a handsome, quiet and unassuming man. When one looked at him and listened to his words, one would conclude that he was not well educated. But that was not the case, for he was a trained weed inspector in the district and was making his rounds past the school grounds bareback on a horse.

This happened during recess several times during the school year and he lingered for a while as the girls rushed to the school yard fence. At the top of their voices they sang an old Scottish song, Charlie is my darling, which they had learned from Miss Schmidt. Charlie rested his horse a little longer and never batted an eye.

The girls' parents never heard about these incidents for they would not have been pleased and the girls would have been forbidden to indulge in such silliness for they were making fun of a professional. In fact, it bothered David that he had been part of such buffoonery, and at Charlie's expense.

When he was older, he met Charlie on the street and introduced himself as one who had sung that Scottish song. He was a bit remorseful, but Charlie told him that he looked forward to that part of his job and enjoyed the singing and the attention he got. After that meeting, David's previous frivolous behavior didn't bother him any longer.

BOX SOCIALS

Miss Schmidt informed her class that something special was going to happen in school on Sunday afternoon. She was planning a box social in order to raise money for much-needed library books, ball and bat, and gifts for children at Christmas time. To prepare for that occasion, pupils would ensure that the schoolroom was extra clean, swept, dusted, and papers and books neatly arranged. The desks were set along the four walls creating a large inner space but still permitting some seating.

She sent a note to the mothers to arrange a secret box with items such as pieces of pie and angel food cake fit for the gods, cream puffs light as a feather, great layer cakes and sandwiches, with lemonade, coffee and tea. Miss Schmidt had already arranged for a fiddler and accordionist to play musical interludes.

On the day of the social, the music makers arrived early and welcomed everyone. Women and girls assembled on the right side of the desks; one, nursing a child, had her baby sleep on piles of coats. Louie was the auctioneer of the beautifully decorated boxes in the shapes of wagons, horses, barns, or even shoes, each containing a fancy lunch. However, the boxes were made by anonymous fashioners for the identification appeared only in the interior.

Everyone tried to guess which one Miss Schmidt had prepared. Young men especially wanted to know, for the successful bidder got to eat the lunch with her. Ted gave special smiles to Miss Schmidt, trying to discern which box she had prepared. He made a high bid on one, richly decorated with flowers. Alas, he missed, and lunched with a common farmer's wife. Louie enjoyed the good-natured bantering and bidding.

Ted had missed his fortune but there were other interesting results: a husband paid an exorbitant price for a box, thinking that it was that of his wife; instead. it was that of a grinning, neighbour woman and he delighted to dine with her. This lucky person even dared to suggest that his wife get this special recipe. His wife, instead, scolded him for wasting so much money. "I could easily have baked five pies for that amount!" Quite a bit of money was raised, all in fun, generally.

While parents were engaged in the bidding procedure, some children tried on the scarves, hats and boots. It was stylish fun and a few scarves got tied together.

The party broke up when parents had to go home and milk the cows. If it was too late many cows mooed in the barn and wondered what was taking so long.

JOYFUL CHRISTMAS CONCERT

There was a lot of preparation for the Christmas concert. Dads retrieved saw horses and planks from storage in the old church and assembled them in the school to make a stage. Most households used coal oil lamps which were useful for small rooms. But this area was much larger and so these lamps were not bright enough although reliable and quite simple to operate.

Gasoline mantel lamps were better for Christmas concerts or social gatherings for they were efficient although difficult and dangerous to operate. Suspended from a suitable place on the ceiling, they used high test gasoline and air under pressure. They hissed and sputtered and needed attention every hour. They were a fire hazard for a very tall person or someone carrying an object might hit them. Sometimes they died out and events had to be stopped.

Additional drawbacks were their delicate mantles which could be damaged by perforations or a sudden jar, wrecking these lacy sheaths. It took time to replace them. But in spite of these limitations, there they were ready to operate on that concert night.

Children prepared a play featuring an addled farmer calculating his meager income and his many expenses. This appealed to these agricultural parents and they clapped enthusiastically as the actor beamed and disappeared into the exit.

Miss Schmidt played her guitar to help children sing Christmas carols such as *Ihr Kinderlein Kommet*. Quietly she cautioned tone deaf Roman to participate by not singing but keeping his lips and mouth moving. The fir tree nestled in a pail of water, wax candles inserted into little tin holders clamped to its boughs, affixed perpendicularly to avert a tree fire. Lit candles were always a fire hazard and therefore there was always someone on watch with a pail of water and sand nearby.

"I remember when our tree caught fire," Thelma recalled, "and my mother emptied the coffee pot to put out the flames."

On the tree were Christmas ornaments and ribbons of all colours, homemade decorations: strung popcorn and cranberries and paper garlands ordered from catalogues.

The performing stage was specially decorated. A set of bed sheets formed its curtains, and crepe paper streamers crossed it. Crepe paper also figured in making costumes, for it was versatile, cheap, stretched easily, could be sewn, glued, pinned, pleated, flaunced, or fluffed. There were special gowns and sunbonnets for the play, Little Red Riding Hood, uniforms for soldiers and policemen, curtains for windows and backdrops, pajamas for clowns, black habits for witches, dancing dresses, and black masks for minstrels.

While these props were resilient, they could come apart. Dennis wore a black mask portraying a black person; while dancing, he lost his mask, could not find it but dashed down to the furnace room, blackened his face with coal and returned, a little late in the play's sequence, but black nevertheless. Christmas art welcomed parents to the annual school concert; they beamed with joy when they saw and heard their darlings on stage and gave thunderous applause at the conclusion of each section.

Santa appeared as the concert concluded. He was not very steady on his feet, gave a loud Ho Ho Ho, Merry Christmas, and handed presents to each pupil. He had a special present for Miss Schmidt and his embrace was noticeably protracted.

RADIO BROADCASTS

Home tube radios were common during David's days. Miss Schmidt became excited when the School Unit provided a battery-operated radio-phono combination to every rural school. The Unit indicated that the reason for providing this instrument was its interest in harnessing the potential of radio to support education. This tool made it possible for pupils to listen to Saskatchewan Department of Education's offering of school radio broadcasts on Tuesdays and Fridays. The first program broadcast was a language arts series entitled Highways to Adventure for Grades 5 to 10, and a junior music series for Grades 1 to 4.

In 1945, R. J. Staples joined the Department of Education as supervisor of music and introduced a new kind of music programming which served as a model for classroom instruction. He felt it was important for children to respond to music through free physical movement and through making and playing their own instruments.

For broadcast, he created Making Music Together, and, with Gertrude Murray, worked closely to produce for the primary levels the series, Rhythmic Patterns and Sounds and Songs; for these he worked as script writer, arranger, and commentator. Staples often prepared the students for singing through a series of records for school broadcasts that he wrote, narrated, and produced.

Pupils were attentive to this novel form of education. The radio-phono machine seemed quite complicated and Miss Schmidt had difficulty operating it and sometimes failed altogether as attentive pupils waited. She then sent a note with David to enlist the help of Louie who came the next day and managed to get it working, sometimes using liquid solder to mend the wires.

During one of the broadcast's innovative music programs, a group of students played an ensemble piece with woodwind instruments. Then someone named each instrument, such as a clarinet or an oboe and played it in turn. Staples encouraged each pupil and the school to purchase these instruments. This suggestion was too sophisticated and expensive for Miss Schmidt's school. After all, these pupils had never seen any of these instruments, let alone heard them, although Mis Schmidt played the guitar.

There was a reed organ at the back of the classroom which no one played; it had previously been in St. John's church. Seeming to realize its overreaching suggestions, the program recommended the purchase and use of recorders. Parents bought plastic ones, tonettes, for each pupil and they played them together.

4

Uncle Mike and military service

WHAT MADE A YOUNG man from prairie Saskatchewan volunteer to serve in Canada's army? Uncle Mike was the youngest in a family of 12 children, son of immigrants from Hungary. He always had a sense of adventure, and going to Europe beckoned him. But there was also a sense of purpose, that of doing something meaningful for himself and his country. Not that he wasn't doing something important on the farm.

At first, he considered his elderly parents and their needs, but Tony, two years younger, could fulfill that requirement. In the family brood he had a sense of family life where everyone had a role to play but in the army he sensed his service could be for the common good, for the protection and care of one another. There, he could feel even more connected and useful.

The army community also appealed to him since the many advertisements enticed men, and women, to enlist. In unimaginable spots, they would sleep, eat and fight in small units, an ad stated. They would be regarded as equals. However, Uncle Mike wondered whether he would be considered an enemy alien since his parents emigrated from the Austro-Hungarian Empire. Would he train and then serve only on the home front?

Instead of serving, he thought he could train and then easily receive a deferral from military service. After all, he had elderly dependents, his parents; he was a farmer and could produce for the country; he was not a conscientious objector. But, nevertheless, he was physically and mentally fit for service.

MAPLE CREEK

David got to know Uncle Mike both from the detailed letters he sent from Maple Creek and his basic training, and from the skimpy letters he sent from Europe. He also filled the Louie-Anne family in when he had brief leaves from training.

"Before I left the farm, I considered what I should do to help Canada," Uncle Mike remembered. "I thought of joining the Royal Canadian Mounted Police for their life seemed very exciting and challenging. I talked it over with Dad and he thought that since I liked being free and driving all over the country, that job might suit me very well. But I was more the adventurous type and wanted to travel outside Canada. Maybe I could drive trucks for the army, I mused."

"If you don't get a yellow stripe down your pant as an RCMP officer, avoid getting a yellow stripe down your back in the army," his Dad advised. "Anyway, maybe in the army you could serve in Italy the tenth-century birthplace of your ancestors. Also, I heard that in Canada boys your age now have to serve in the armed forces."

So, Uncle Mike joined up at the basic training field in Maple Creek with his farmer friend, Raymond. Soon they were transferred to Suffield, Alberta, and went through poisonous gas tests, he recalled. They remembered that ordeal very well. Lieutenant Smith talked to them the night before and picked 20 of them and told them that they were going on a trip in the morning, right after 5 o'clock breakfast. "Be in full military dress but don't take any guns."

They were ready when a canvas-covered truck came along and they sat in the box on seats in the front and along the sides. "When we arrived at a hut, we were instructed to put gas masks on and check them whether they were working properly. Then they released a blue gas fog. So, we walked around in that gas. Then the officer told us, 'Okay, take your finger and lift the mask and take a whiff of the gas.'

"Well, I must have taken too much of a whiff for that stuff hit me and burnt like extra hot coffee all the way down my pipe. We were told that it was chlorine gas which we might experience on the war front.

"Then we were marched to another hut, were handed a damp towel and were told to strip to the waist. Two officers came along and sprayed mustard gas on our arms and shoulders and instructed us that when it started to burn, we could wipe it off. And it burnt good. We weren't allowed to wash it off for two days. Then the officer looked us right in the eyes and said, 'You are on a secret mission and if any word of this gets out, you'll be shot on the spot.'

"But my health was almost ruined after those poisonous gas tests. I got mumps on both sides and then double pneumonia. Then I got scarlet fever and my throat was so raw I could speak only in a whisper. I had to be hospitalized, but I recovered, although I lost feeling in my left leg and my toenails fell off. I had to bathe my leg for a long time and my foot was coated in blood.

"We also went to a school of sorts. We had to become qualified in elementary subjects such as drill, physical training, first aid, marching, small arms and gas training, field craft, and map reading. I enjoyed firing on the rifle range and was rated an above-average shot. Then I was posted to the Advanced Infantry Training Centre for nine weeks; we engaged in physical marching, bayonet fighting, judging distance, digging and wiring, field training and sub-machine gun usage.

"In his lectures to us, Captain Gung-ho, as we called him among ourselves, talked about high standards in the army. We knew he was a Saturday-night soldier with no experience of active army life. His perfectionist eye focused on our boots and belts, bars and buttons, and especially the white patch we wore on our corps or regimental badges.

"We tried to tame Captain Gung-ho by beating him at his own game. Raymond and I started to outdo him by following closely behind him on grueling cross-country runs to make him run faster and faster. Eventually he had to surrender the lead.

"Everyone entering the service was given standardized tests to ascertain his abilities and determine in which area he might serve. I had some knowledge of trucks, cars and tractors on the farm and received high marks simply because I knew something about engine compression and amperes. I was assigned to the motor repair department even though I had barely finished grade school.

"Another officer, George, gave us talks about poison gas warfare. He brought up crazy stories about how Russian kids frustrated the German army by peeing in their gas tanks and putting dinner plates on the roads to give a crackling sound like land mines.

"He gave us some advice about two types of information agents; one, he said, were authentic sources which relied on allied and resistance documents, a source which he reluctantly called white propaganda, and another, which he immediately labeled black propaganda, were enemy sources.

"He also added some inside data about home-made explosives which could target enemy factory machinery, railroad lines and other means of transportation, dock installations, commerce, shipping, telecommunications, grounded aircraft, berthed submarines, and other naval ships.

"Our barracks were flimsy shacks with primitive facilities. But there was a second barrack where we could study and eat and bond with one another. The food was abundant and well prepared and served by young ladies from the women's army. As long as we were here, our uniforms, haircuts and housekeeping habits were no longer under constant scrutiny. A young private ran his hand up the inside of our waitress's thigh as she leaned over the table to remove a dish. She screamed bloody murder. He was gone by the next meal.

"Raymond and I were getting fed up by all this regimentation and rules. We decided to just take off, knowing that there were penalties for being absent without leave. We did not want to stay away too long because then we would be regarded as deserters and there would be more dire penalties.

"There was not much to do in the town of Maple Creek, however, but we could walk wherever we wanted and order a beer. As we returned, we approached the camp gate and the guard asked for our passes. When he learned that we did not have any, he took us to the guard house and locked us up. We were surprised that this place was full, for many others had been away without leave.

"In the morning two armed guards paraded us before the colonel. We were sentenced to two weeks of barracks confinement as well as the loss of one month's pay and passes. In our confinement we spent an hour scrubbing floors each evening.

GUINEA PIG CLUB

"After we finished basic training, Raymond and I were sent overseas to England. During our stay there, our Canadian company visited Victoria Hospital, a cottage treatment centre in East Grinstead, West Sussex. Here war victims had reconstructive surgery performed by military doctors. Some patients had serious skin burns, others had lost fingers and legs.

"Richard, one of the residents who fought in the Battle of Britain, gave us a tour and a history of the hospital. His face was scarred when his Spitfire airplane was downed by German fighters."

"All of us who have war engraved on our hands and faces are members of the Guinea Pig Club," Richard stated. "One of us who has no fingers is secretary, so the minutes of meetings are really short. Another member who lost both legs is our treasurer for he certainly can't run off with our cash.

"You will notice that I have stubs for my ears and so I have a hard time keeping my glasses on. I lost much of my nose, sweat glands, hair and nipples. I still had some skin under my armpits, lower belly and groin. My eyelids melted away and my eyeballs bulged out. My lips were pulled back, baring my teeth. I was a mess, but now I have monstrous good looks! My hands are gnarled but I can move my fingers a little and my pinkies are webbed to the next finger, an overgrowth from the healing process.

"I can do a lot of things with my hands, but I have to put them together to turn a door knob. I don't mind telling you that. Our Boss gave me upper eyelids from my foreskin for it is thin, soft and stretchy. He used skin from my scrotum to rebuild my lower lids. Our Boss also used skin from cadavers.

"I should tell you that the person I refer to as the Boss is Dr. Archibald McIndoe who is in charge of helping us get back to normal. He refers to us as guinea pigs because he likes to try new healing methods on us and so all of us are members of the Guinea Pig Club."

The name, Guinea Pig, indicated the experimental nature of the reconstructive work practiced on the Club's members and the new equipment designed specifically to treat these injuries. Originally, those of the Royal Air Force (RAF) who had gone through at least 10 surgical procedures and were patients of Dr. McIndoe formed this Club. Most fighter pilots from the Bomber Command who had severe burns were British but other significant minorities included Canadians.

"I have some memories of the ordeal in my fiery airplane," Richard continued. "My skin seemed to be bubbling, shrinking and tightening. I could smell my hair and clothes burning. In fact, when I crashed, I jumped out and rolled in the grass and it caught fire. I wondered whether I really wanted to live.

"The grafts of skin I received went on and on and were very painful. Dr. McIndoe thought there should be a much faster way of growing skin.

"A young child was visiting here the other day and when he saw me he asked if I was a volcano explorer. I loved that."

McIndoe had to deal with very severe injuries but had hope for recovery because these men were so young. He improved, developed and invented many techniques for treating, reconstructing and rehabilitating burn casualties, for the treatment of burns by surgery was in its infancy. Before that time, many severely burned casualties would not have survived.

Richard led the Canadian soldiers to a ward filled with recovering airmen. "I want to point out air gunner Les who lost most of his face and hands. He doesn't mind our talking about him in his presence. He is getting better even though he is swaddled head to toe in bandages and is heavily sedated. We should visit only at a distance for his unhealed skin means that he is open to infection. Our Boss had to recreate his fingers by making incisions between his knuckles. Others have burns that need several surgical operations that take many years to heal."

"Now I myself am suffering because of the war," Les whispered. "I never realized the suffering I was causing when I was up 30,000 feet. I did not hear the screams nor smell the blood of those losing limbs and eyes. I did not really know what bomber pilots do."

"What's really important for us Guinea Pigs," Richard said, "is that our Boss makes the long hospital stay for his boys, as he calls us, a relaxed one. He works so that we disfigured ones can eventually carry on in a more or less normal fashion.

"As you can see, our life in this military hospital is not very different from regular life for we wear ordinary clothes instead of hospital blues. We also can leave the hospital whenever we want. I'll take you to another ward where there are barrels of beer and a piano to encourage an informal and happy atmosphere and make sure that we drink enough liquids, which we do all right!"

Many residents in Victoria Hospital were victims of accidents with Hurricane and Spitfire war planes. Both the Hurricanes and Spitfires had powerful engines that gave them the speed they needed during air battles. The Hurricane, a short-range, high performance interceptor aircraft, was most effective against enemy bombers. It provided the pilot with good all-round visibility since the cockpit was mounted reasonably high in the fuselage, creating a distinctive hump-back silhouette.

"But as we were flying," Richard said, "we had nowhere to go but down. I found out that our shelf-life was 11 days as a pilot. It was really a hellish time."

In the Battle of Britain, the Spitfire became the backbone of the RAF Fighter Command. Much loved by its pilots, it served in many roles: as interceptor, photo-reconnaissance, fighter-bomber, carrier-based fighter, and trainer. Unarmed, the Spits could carry two vertical cameras and one oblique one mounted in the rear fuselage. As photo reconnaissance, this aircraft provided an almost continual flow of valuable intelligence information.

The most widely produced and strategically important British single-seat fighter during the war, the Spitfire gave exceptional performance and air superiority at high altitudes. Fighter-bomber versions could transport a 250- or 500-pound bomb beneath the fuselage and a 250-pound bomb under each wing.

Powered by high octane aviation fuel, both the Hurricane and the Spitfire carried considerable quantities of this highly inflammable liquid. If one of the fighters caught fire—which was a common occurrence if hit by enemy fire—the flames spread quickly throughout the plane, causing horrible burn injuries to the pilot and erasing many faces.

"The Boss treats pilots with deep burns," Richard again recalled. "He provides early skin grafts to make sure we can function and suffer the least disfigurement. He's quite the experimenter and some of us have had dozens of operations. One of his big enemies is graft rejection," Richard said.

During the Battle of Britain, 35 horribly burnt fighter pilots were sent to McIndoe for treatment. Standard treatment for serious burns at this time was to cover the wounds with tannic acid in order to dry the affected area and allow removal of the dead skin. Unfortunately, this process was extremely painful and left patients with extensive scarring.

McIndoe was convinced there was a better solution. Noting that burnt pilots who bailed out into the sea were less scarred than others, he started bathing patients in saline. This proved a much gentler treatment process, with the saline solution lessening healing times and increasing survival rates for patients with extensive burns. McIndoe and his crew operated on these human war wreckages using their meticulous skills of cutting, grafting, and stitching.

"What we really appreciate about the Boss is what he did for us psychologically," Richard said. "He repaired not only our faces but our minds and spirits as well. We thought we had done something well-nigh heroic for our country, but most people could not bear the sight of our awful scars. We recovering warriors felt that those we had tried to help were now rejecting us. We were shot down once, and now were being shot down again.

"The Boss bent hospital rules and asked townspeople to take us as we were. So, we are exhilarated when families invite us into their homes for meals and to visit. We are no longer hidden away and made to feel isolated but are welcome in pubs and dance halls. But that takes some getting used to.

"The Boss regularly joins us in social events inside the hospital, takes us out for drinks, and encourages us to associate with community members," Richard noted. "We like to blend in as much as possible. Some people are scared of us and I understand that. The high moment for me was when a person thanked me for not hiding.

"These socializing results are amazing. There are now some loving relationships between patients and nurses, and with women in town. So, we are beginning to feel better not only about our faces but also about our whole selves. We feel celebrated. I know that war brings out the worst in people, but I am experiencing the best. East Grinstead happily is becoming the town that does not stare. This helped us pick up our lives.

"We cannot hide completely the ugly faces of war, but the Boss is someone who takes our broken faces and makes new ones for us. He also creates places where we can go without embarrassment. To those who are discharged into civilian life he often loans money.

"As a conclusion to our visit, let me sing you our Guinea Pig Anthem to the tune of Aurelia by Sam Wesley:

> We are McIndoe's army,
> We are his Guinea Pigs.
> With dermatomes and pedicles,
> Glass eyes, false teeth and wigs.
> And when we get our discharge
> We'll shout with all our might:
> Per ardua ad astra. [To the stars with strong determination.]
> We'd rather drink than fight
> John Hunter runs the gas works,
> Ross Tilley wields the knife.
> And if they are not careful
> They'll have your flaming life.
> So, Guinea Pigs, stand ready
> For all your surgeon's calls:
> And if their hands aren't steady
> They'll whip off both your ears
> We've had some mad Australians,
> Some French, some Czechs, some Poles.
> We've even had some Yankees,
> God bless their precious souls.
> While as for the Canadians—
> Ah! That's a different thing.
> They couldn't stand our accent
> And built a separate Wing
> We are McIndoe's army.

David remembered the letters sent to his family, labelled, L86615, Uncle Mike's as a private in the 8th Army. Some of the letters were censored with portions blackened out. In all of them Uncle Mike showed some measure of reserve. The first letters were from the training section in Maple Creek, as noted earlier. Here Uncle Mike was very excited about the war effort and his contribution to it.

He acknowledged all the letters sent to him in Europe. "Thank you for all the letters you sent me. I always waited for them and sometimes it took 90 days for them to arrive. That's why I asked that your letters be sent by airmail. Part of the reason for delays was that we were constantly moving around, especially in Sicily."

Louie hired Aboriginal men to work on the farm especially during harvest time. Most of them stooked the bundles of wheat and oats. One of them, George, was a war veteran and he shared his stories of the war.

"I volunteered for the war and peace keeping," he stated. "I welcomed the opportunity to escape from Reserve life. My community put on quite a show to send me off, a ceremonial council dance, gifts of a pipe, a medicine bundle of herbs and a small drum as physical and spiritual powers. The pipe stem hidden under my shirt, it turned out, deflected a deadly bullet. When I communicated with my animal, the bear, he gave me strength and guidance.

"I remember that in the war we, the red soldiers among the white, were treated as equals. I was an expert in thwarting the Germans by blowing up bridges. I sang traditional songs for burials and gave a war whoop in times of danger. I remember the sights, sounds and smells of war for it inflicted much suffering. There were my wounded comrades, seeing my friends die, feeling shell shock and realizing the effects of friendly fire.

"My family was anxious while I was away and they sat around the radio awaiting news of me. They tried to remain close to me through prayers and ceremonies at home.

"On my return there was a powwow celebration, giving of an eagle feather and a headdress befitting a brave warrior. Fellow veterans smudged me and my family. Rejoicing continued in the form of dancing, drumming and singing. From the government, I received medals for my war effort. In the face of the tremendous adversity of war, my Native culture was the source of strength and healing.

"But there were negative reactions also. I remember that on my return, I tried to reintegrate into my community; at first, I was rejected by fellow Indians and non-Indians alike and received unfair and unequal treatment for loans and land sales. Even now several years after the war, the memories and consequences of the war persist such as headaches, nightmares and the feeling of isolation. Some call me a coward because I find it hard to cope and function in my community. I am grateful, however, that my elders gave me counseling and support to manage these symptoms. Several sweat lodges that I attended also helped me."

ITALIAN CAMPAIGN

Back to Uncle Mike. He and Raymond set sail from England to Sicily. En route, Uncle Mike learned a little about that part of Italy. It had been occupied by many powers for it held a strategic position between Europe and North Africa. Whoever ruled Sicily could maneuver between these two continents and control the Mediterranean basin.

In 1860 Garibaldi helped annex this island into the new kingdom of Italy. The allies now wanted to dominate over Sicily and over all of Italy and thereby control the direction of the war.

"We were told that the country was rugged, with the malarial mosquito flourishing in the hot lowlands and the enemy controlling the high ground," Uncle Mike noted. "This high ground and the mountain backbone was an obvious advantage to the defenders. Roads were seldom level and rarely straight. We were in for some fierce and challenging battles."

There was a lot of wheat growing, which Uncle Mike could relate to. But life for the Sicilian peasant was a harsh and constant struggle.

BUG DETAIL

Although a private in the army, Uncle Mike received specialized training. He had never heard such well-researched lectures. Instructor Walter began by examining infectious diseases in general. He read from the Handbook of Military Hygiene: "There are no subjects of greater importance than the preservation of the health of the soldier and the prevention of disease in the army."

Walter emphasized that diseases took such a great toll on military personnel; they not only limited or rendered ineffective the fighting ability of individual soldiers, but were also a drain on the army's materials and resources. Treating sick casualties consumed the efforts of others and led to the expenditure of scarce energy and supplies needed to conduct military operations.

Uncle Mike wrote: "We were told that not just enemy guns, but an unseen enemy, infectious diseases, threatened us and could cause casualties greater than the entire war. Body lice and rats often carried the diseases."

"While we are preparing for a campaign we can keep diseases under control," Walter said. "The greater challenge is to prevent diseases during a campaign. First, field soldiers might experience lowered resistance to disease due to a lack of and/or poor quality of sleep, food, and protection from the elements. Second, cross infection between soldiers can be facilitated by frequently crowded conditions.

"Third, sanitation facilities which were normally taken for granted by civilians and soldiers during peace time had to be rudimentarily recreated in the field. Last, it was often militarily expedient to cross or inhabit areas in which some diseases naturally flourished."

Instructor Walter was especially eloquent on the subject of malaria. It had shaped the course of human history for a long time, controlled the movement of wars and countries' economies. Kings, popes, and military leaders often succumbed to malaria in the prime of their lives: Alexander the Great in fourth century, B.C., Dante Alighieri in the 14th A.D., and Oliver Cromwell in the 17th.

"Malaria and typhus, with its brothers and sisters—plague, cholera, typhoid, dysentery—have decided more wars than Caesar, Hannibal, Napoleon, and all generals. In fact, many times armies were prevented from entering a country because of the presence of malaria. Often, more soldiers died from it than from combat. Armies themselves were often to be blamed for the spread of the disease since they created thousands of breeding places for mosquitoes.

"Only the female anopheles mosquito sucks blood and becomes a deadly predator," Walter stated. "She begins with an ominous tiny whine that hones around your ear just after you've gotten comfortable in your sleeping bag. To protect Italians, especially farmers, Mussolini drained the swamps. The male mosquito, by way of contrast, lives a contented, short, gentle adult life like a swallowtail butterfly, sipping nectar from flowers.

"But the mosquito ladies have an excuse," Walter continued. "Being (most of them) good mothers, they are biting to provide food for their babies. The problem, I suppose, is that they have a great many babies. A female mosquito in a full lifetime will lay about 10 separate batches of eggs, roughly 200 in a batch. For that, the mother needs blood, your blood. So, I'm sure you (or some of you) can find it in your hearts to forgive her.

"Well, most of you like to preserve a rich diversity of animal species and you appreciate the large tracts of equatorial rain forest. Such a diversity has defended the last outposts of ferns, butterflies, beetles and ants from destructive humankind. But you jungle lovers also have to take care, for this blood-sucking lady mosquito is in that jungle and is willing to bite to defend her turf. And give you that disease. Therefore, explorers and exploiters had to back off and so unwittingly these blood suckers staved off human exploitation of the forest.

"We have two enemies, two divisions preventing victory: malaria, and the Nazis. It's your job to attack and eliminate both."

The buzz word in these talks was control, for the whole army was in a state of vigilance about the mosquitoes' breeding places.

"Parasites develop in the gut of the female mosquito," Walter continued, "and are nourished by each blood meal. When she bites, her saliva with the parasites enters the victim's blood; the parasites enter the liver where they invade the cells, multiply and break down red blood cells. This induces bouts of fever and anemia in the infected individual and damages vital organs leading to the death of the patient."

Walter tried to inject some humor into his lesson. "If you are sleeping in an infested area and don't take preventive measures, the only way to avoid them is to determine which are male and which are female, for only females transmit the disease. So, you need a great pair of binoculars to determine their sex. Especially if you are sleeping.

"Newer anti-malaria drugs are coming into use all the time, including the natural ingredient, quinine. Although it has a bitter taste (many patients vomit after taking it), it has fever-reducing and pain-killing properties. It is made from the bark of the cinchona tree.

"In the 17th century, the Quechua Indians of Peru and Bolivia discovered its healing properties and now Dutch plantations in Java produce most of the world's supply of cinchona bark. But this supply was cut off when the Germans conquered the Netherlands. Soon synthetic anti-malarial drugs and residual insecticides like DDT were available. DDT was first used to kill clothes moths, mosquitoes and houseflies.

"Soldiers must encamp in safe locations free from mosquitoes," Walter stated. "Also, many species of anophelines have different breeding habits. All develop only in water, but some prefer specific locations: rice paddies, pools and puddles, foothill running streams, swamps or ponds, marshes, wells, fresh water or brackish, and sun, or shade. Therefore, malaria control requires the help of trained personnel who know or can find the habitats of the mosquitoes."

"All of us liked to attend movies in the evening," Uncle Mike wrote. "But we found out that most mosquitoes feed only at this time. So, we had to protect ourselves from these night-biting creatures. Also, we had to screen our sleeping quarters."

"Actually, it should be easier to control malaria in the army than in regular life," Walter observed. "Here the commanding officer is in complete control; all of us have the same living habits and lots of anti-malaria funds and supplies. But we have to be careful in other ways; army living does not necessarily mean sanitary conditions, but focuses on efforts to control life and death and not the mosquitoes. Also, we spend a lot of time working at night. Thus, troops may be exposed to the malaria incidence more often than normal for the area.

"Trenches, foxholes, tank traps, gun emplacements, vehicle ruts, shell, bomb and mine craters, sabotaged irrigation projects, streams ponded by bridge rubble and improvised causeways, drainage blocked by hastily built airfields and highways—all may provide additional breeding places for malaria mosquitoes."

Walter used many words to make everyone conscious of malaria. "Training and education of both medical and line officers in regard to malaria and its control are essential. Malaria control in the army is a military problem. A malaria policy must not only be formulated; it must be enforced. Malaria discipline is absolutely necessary to an army's success. Don't be forgetful.

"There are many who are in charge of sanitary duties. But this is not sufficient. You are part of a necessary unity to survey, plan, execute, supervise, and maintain the numerous and technical measures that must be carried out continuously if malaria is to be defeated. You need to give it full and undivided attention. The prevention of malaria is neither automatic nor simple.

"Besides the remedies of quinine and DDT, there is atabrine. One tablet a day prevents overt attacks of malaria, curing those infected, and postponing clinical manifestations of infections until the drug is withheld. Our forces could then fight in highly malarious surroundings without being hampered by clinical malaria.

"Atabrine's continued use usually causes a yellow colouring of the skin. This has no harmful effects, however, and soon disappears when the drug is discontinued. Anti-malarial drugs such as atabrine kill the parasite and alleviate the symptoms of fever, shivering, pain in the joints and head-ache. Cases of severe disease including cerebral malaria, however, require hospital care." Walter also gave a brief history of the treatment of malaria. "Fevers have always haunted humans and they have tried several remedies to combat them. The ancients tried blood-letting, vomiting, amputation, skull operations, opium and opium-laced beer. Many remedies sought to expel bad air (hence the name mal- aria) or swamp gases or poisons from the body. Treatments even sought the help of astrology as the cycle of ma-larial fevers suggested a connection with astronomical events. Egyptians used preventative measures such as sleeping in tower-like structures or under nets in swampy areas.

"There were many strange remedies: allowing the insects to devour 77 small cakes made from a dough prepared by mixing flour and patient's urine was one; another was letting the matron of a noble family cut the ear of a cat, add three drops of its blood to brandy along with some pep-per, and administer it to the patient. Rubbing the patient's body with chips from a gallows on which a criminal had been recently executed was another method. But no one found an effective cure and people continued to die.

"The expansion of agricultural methods and the rise in population density contributed to the spread of malaria. As forests were cleared, new areas opened up for breeding mosquitoes."

As noted before, one of the largest combined operations of World War II was the invasion of Sicily. When the struggle was over, Sicily was the first area to fall to Allied forces. Near the toe of Italy, it was both a base for the invasion of that country and a training ground for many of the officers and enlisted men.

In his letters home, Uncle Mike was not specific as to the area he was serving but indicated he was "somewhere in Sicily" or "somewhere in Italy." These letters were general enough that they were stamped on the outside as having been passed by the censor.

"I hope the war is soon over," Uncle Mike wrote as allied forces penetrated Italy. "Maybe the war-weary Italians will drop out of the war altogether."

He noted that Italy provided an ideal area for the Germans and Mus-solini. The central mountains, the Apennines, rise about 10,000 feet and

have offshoots that run east and west toward the coast. There are deep val-
leys containing wide rivers flowing rapidly to the sea. Bridges guard the
north-south roads.

"There, I hoped to find military action, active front-line duty," Uncle
Mike wrote, "but was disappointed for, instead, I was assigned to the malaria control unit. Then I had to help curb venereal disease. It seemed I could
not escape this bug business. But I will write more on that detail later."

As part of the bug squad, as he called it, Uncle Mike helped enforce
very strict measures to control the mosquitoes. A large anti-malarial unit
covered the expansive areas of Sicily and Italy. There were several methods
of control. One was to limit or eradicate the mammals, birds, insects that
transmit the disease. Another strategy included the control of the mosquitoes' habitat and the use of chemical and biological means to ensure that
there were no infections and if so to control them.

The main control for such an area was to mix one shovel of lime and
Paris Green arsenic with 50 shovels of sand and spread this over all the pools
of water within half a mile of the camp. There were many eggs and larvae in
the muddy water that often collected in hoof prints and wheel ruts.

"This way of controlling the pests involved a lot of hand work," Uncle
Mike wrote. Open ground spraying often kept the area free of adult mosquitoes. Aerial spraying of large tracts of land with DDT was tested in the
latter stages of the war, but it was not perfected by the British and, therefore,
not widely used.

A faster method of controlling the mosquitoes was that of using an
airplane to dust streams and other breeding places. When the larvae came
up for air, they sucked in this poison and died.

A not-too-bright corporal who supervised one such operation did not
warn the villagers of the operation. When their cattle drank the water in the
control area, they keeled over and died. The buzzards came to clean up the
environment and they also died. Since many villagers made their gourmet
meals from these North African vultures, the local hospital was full of very
sick people.

Of course, soldiers could slap and crush the mosquitoes with their
hands. Other local and minor methods included the use of hand-held units
to spray an insecticide of pyrethrum and coal oil on interior walls, floors
and ceilings, and contents (benches, cots, tables, etc.). To aid the finding of
mosquitoes and the spraying of one's quarters, walls in barracks or buildings

were painted in light colours to contrast with the mosquitoes. These aerosol methods were used just before a battalion left the lines for their rest period.

Immediately after leaving the line, each member of a battalion had precedence at the baths where they presented their entire kit, all clothing, including underclothes and socks, blankets and coats for disinfection. The clothing on the men's backs was chemically treated and returned to each man upon the completion of his bath, along with a fresh suit of under-clothing and socks, with the rest of their items forwarded to them after being properly laundered and dried. While these men were bathing, those soldiers heading back for the line would clean and spray their lodgings with the same coal oil solution used in trench dug-outs.

An important anti-malarial precaution was the prevention of cross-infection, that is, stopping mosquitoes from transporting the malaria parasite from an infected and sick soldier to a healthy soldier. This measure was often easy to accomplish since those afflicted with malaria were usually exhausted and bed-ridden.

Based on the British model, each combat or medical unit formed a small anti-malaria squad under the direction of the group's anti-malaria officer. The squad's role was to carry out anti-mosquito measures in areas immediately adjacent to its encampments. Related tasks could range from overturning discarded tin cans to draining small marshes.

Outdoor application of insecticides aimed at killing mosquitoes in the larvae stage. Anti-Malaria Control Units assumed this highly specialized and large-scale task to eliminate or treat mosquito breeding areas, and the eradication of larvae and adults.

One such innovation arose out of the need to kill mosquito larvae in drinking water, and yet keep the water potable. In such cases, a small amount of gasoline was added to the unit's water barrels. A guard was then posted to ensure that this now tainted water was not consumed for a 24-hour period, during which the gas would evaporate and the water would again be rendered drinkable.

Insecticide was popular on the black market. Civilians often surround-ed soldiers to beg for quinine. Many Italians eagerly traded fresh chicken eggs with Canadian soldiers for flit, a brand name for an insecticide. This original product, launched in 1923 and mainly intended for killing flies and mosquitoes, was mineral oil.

Pamphlets gave information on malaria control and reiterated that a battle, even a campaign, could be lost without a bullet being fired. The most common enemy is this local inhabitant who has glorious opportunities for a feast since his prey is generally half-clad and does not use a mosquito net at night. Posters for malaria control featured a sleeping soldier's sleeves rolled up, exposing his body to mosquito bites.

Malaria was so widespread in Sicily that besides chemical intervention there were strict and enforced rules for the army. Soldiers had to take their anti-malaria tablets daily and be fully dressed at sundown. With these protective measures, authorities then judged there was no reason for contracting malaria. In fact, reporting sick with malaria could be a chargeable offence.

For those who contracted malaria, the cure was terrible. Four days of taking atabrine, four days of mepacrine and another four of straight quinine. What a horrible taste even when followed by boiled sugar water! In low suppressive doses, quinine did not protect individuals from being bitten and having the malaria parasite introduced into their blood, but it did serve to keep the malaria parasite in check and prevented the spread of the disease. Large doses of quinine were reserved for treatment of full-blown cases of malaria, since the drug could be toxic and, if not administered carefully, could cause permanent liver damage.

"The weather was very hot and at night there were millions of mosquitoes trying to bite us," Uncle Mike recalled. "I used to put my plastic gas cape over me but it was too hot and when I took it off the mosquitoes got to me. But I was taking anti-malaria pills. I didn't know I had malaria, but one night on guard duty I was sweating and had a terrible headache and a fellow Canadian took over from me and told me to go to the hospital.

"They said I had malaria and put me on a hospital ship going to Malta. It was an awful journey and as the ship was full of insects it was a tremendous relief to see Malta, south of Sicily. All the quinine had gone so they starved me for two weeks with just cups of tea to drink and eventually the malaria died down."

Many times, highly motivated soldiers did not seek medical care for infectious diseases. Although ailing, some soldiers wanted to tough it out so as to not be taken out of the fight and/or be separated from their comrades-in-arms. Other soldiers avoided seeking treatment to better conform to the gender ideal of manliness, not wanting to perceive themselves or be perceived as being soft.

In some of these cases, this tactic resulted in maintaining an effective fighting force, because some minor sicknesses required nothing but time to cure. Unfortunately, these avoidance practices could result in the needless propagation of the disease via cross-infection, and/or an individual sol-dier's untreated illness could eventually develop or transform into a larger and more serious problem.

PRETENDERS

Medical officers also had to deal with suspected pretenders who feigned illness in order to get a short break from the rigors of trench life or to dodge their military duties altogether. Such shirkers intentionally wounded them-selves or intentionally exposed themselves to an infectious disease.

"My friend, Raymond, was not a pretender," Uncle Mike noted. "He suffered shell shock and began to act strange after his round of duty on the front. He had crippling wounds that did not show. Was he too close to exploding shells? But staff and nurses who were not near exploding shells often reported similar symptoms. Both Raymond and I had begun with romantic ideas of war, and we remembered the cheers that sent us off. Now his symptoms were bewildering: inability to sleep, nightmares, headaches, and shaking. It was odd to see him curl up like a baby in the womb when-ever a loud noise sounded.

"Both of us thought we were tough combatants. But we also had to acknowledge that there were forces beyond our control. In the trenches we were stuck in the muck and mud. We experienced pitiless bombardment where explosives reduced men to particles so small that the wind carried them away.

"I saw so many broken faces. One shell buried the dead and another uncovered them again. We were constantly on edge with a high level of desperation. Some of us felt like asking for a leave, but we felt unmanlike and sheepish, shirking our duty.

"Raymond had no family history of mental illness. I discussed his condition of shell shock with him. He was obviously not pretending; he was not a weak character. We heard that some hard-line military leaders did not believe in this nervous exhaustion and gave drastic punishments like court-martials or death by a firing squad. In their precarious situations, men like Raymond were sent back to the front lines. They could not be good soldiers, however. To preserve their lives and avoid institutionaliza-tion in a mental hospital such men often deserted, but survived.

"It seemed as if Raymond should be hospitalized but he did not have any physical wounds."

"I can't do this anymore!" he pleaded.

"Military personnel sometimes believed that farmers like Raymond and me should be used to this process because we routinely killed either farm animals or wild ones for food. They thought we would always be strong and courageous.

"So desperate was one Canadian soldier, one of his comrades observed, that he scrounged around the incinerator and found a can of beef which had spoiled. To eat it meant poisoning, but he was willing to take a chance because it meant going to a hospital and getting away from it all. His nerves could stand it no longer. Were soldiers such as these cowards? Not at all. Some of these men had proven their bravery time after time. They were simply fed up."

There were abuses in the military. One was that of excessive alcohol consumption on the battle field, during active duty, and, later, at home. At the military base, Raymond felt along with many of his fellow soldiers that holding one's liquor was akin to being a real soldier. This was on a par with knowing how to handle his weapon. Heavy drinking was often glamorized among those in uniform. It provided a moment of recreation and a release from the stresses of battle, being removed from loved ones, and boredom.

Military doctors had divided opinions about allowing alcohol, for some saw its use as a justified morale-boosting measure assuaging discontent, whereas others saw it as harmful to health and performance. Those advocating alcohol consumption noted its medicinal benefits; rum, for instance, could both feed, warm and also serve as a stimulant. The difficulty was to strike a balance between reasonable and excessive consumption in situations of extreme hazard.

A song that struck a bittersweet note with Uncle Mike and his fellows was I'll be Home for Christmas. He hoped it would be so, even though it ended with If only in my dreams. He had in mind Vera Lynn's We'll meet again when he wrote home and to his siblings.

The battlefield experience often accompanied combatants on leave and upon discharge. Raymond would have to sleep alone at home and awakened in a panic and struggle to get back to sleep. The battleground also attended him during the day. Car horns shattered his nerves. He had unexpected flashbacks at the whiff of cleaning chemicals. Remarks of a minor nature led to fights during domestic times. He attacked his brother over the brand of beer he purchased.

Uncle Mike revealed only bits and pieces of his army life in his letters to his brother Louie and to David and Theresa. Even so, military intelligence censored some of these outlines, seemingly of details of precise location, and past and future battle information.

At home he was not very detailed either. "I had lived the war and tried to bury it when I went home, but sometimes I recalled a few incidents only to bury them again. So, I had at least two burials."

VD CONTROL

Since Uncle Mike had done such a good job in anti-malaria control, he was moved to the venereal disease (VD) unit, another position he had not bargained for. Chaplains, surgeons and privates attended lectures on the diseases of gonorrhea and syphilis. Since the beginning of military actions, sexual hygiene and behavior had been a problem. Male soldiers were often lonely, had time to spare, were homesick and were looking for female companionship.

The VD classes emphasized education and protection: these diseases can be prevented; they are caught by sexual contact with an infected woman; all prostitutes and pick-ups are probably infected; the only 100 percent way to avoid venereal diseases is to avoid sexual contact. Crossing your fingers won't prevent venereal good-time girls from infecting, nor will crossing their legs prevent unwanted pregnancies, but a rubber might if it covers the infected areas. A good soldier will not get this disease, for contracting it will aid the axis powers.

In this war, raised awareness reduced lost services due to VD; there was information about VD's dangers and advancements in treatments. But still infection was a cost to the armed forces because of lost time from duty and diversion of medical resources.

To strengthen the message of the lectures, matchbooks in ration cartons had catchy slogans warning against the dangers of VD. There were also films and posters, striking slogans and warnings urging men to embrace their patriotic pride, faithfulness to loved ones at home and personal self-interest to avoid sexual contact.

Pamphlets emphasized that manhood comes from healthy sex organs. "It is not necessary to have sexual intercourse in order to keep strong and well. Since you have a healthy body now, keep it that way. Stay away from easy women; don't gamble your health away. Use safety measures. If you get diseased, report at once to your commanding officer. Time is most important. Will power and self-control help to keep a man's body and mind healthy. A healthy body and a healthy mind lead to happiness."

Uncle Mike displayed these posters with their hard-hitting messages. In his regiment, treatment was free but not always confidential. There was some form of punishment for contracting the disease such as a deduction in pay and loss of privileges. Infected cooks were forbidden to handle food until all traces of the disease were gone. Uncle Mike also handed out kits so individuals could begin their treatments.

In the lectures, combatants learned that these sexually transmitted diseases were named venereal after Venus, the Greek goddess of love. Gonorrhea is caused by a bacterium. Its symptoms are a yellowish discharge from the penis. There may also be pain or burning during urination.

Women may notice a vaginal discharge and painful urination. They may also experience pain in the lower abdomen and/or bleeding between periods or after sexual intercourse. Pregnant women can pass the disease to an unborn child. Babies born with gonorrhea can be blind. One important note though is that some infected individuals are without symptoms.

Uncle Mike also listened to talks on syphilis, a disease called the great imitator, for its symptoms are like those of other diseases. It is passed on through contact with a syphilis sore. Sores occur mainly on the external genitals, vagina, anus, or in the rectum. Sores can also occur on the lips and in the mouth.

Transmission of the syphilis organism occurs during vaginal, anal, or oral sex. Its symptoms vary with the four stages of the disease. The first symptom is a non-itchy ulcer that leaks a clear contagious liquid, with flu-like symptoms; the next stage shows a diffuse rash which might involve the palms of the hands and soles of the feet, chest, arms and legs; the third stage might involve no symptoms, and during the last stage the bacteria enter the nervous system, bones and heart. Because syphilis sores can be hidden in the vagina, rectum, or mouth, it may not be obvious that a sex partner has syphilis.

There are possible complications of syphilis: brain damage resulting in changes of mood, muscle weakness and loss of movement; heart and blood vessel damage; irreversible eye damage resulting in blindness, fever, swollen lymph glands, sore throat, patchy hair loss, headaches, weight loss, muscle aches, and fatigue.

The surest way to avoid transmission of sexually transmitted diseases, including syphilis, is to abstain from sexual contact or to be in a long-term mutually monogamous relationship with a partner who has been tested and is known to be uninfected.

Alcohol and drugs may lead to risky sexual behavior and its avoidance can help prevent transmission of syphilis.

Any unusual discharge, sore, or rash, particularly in the groin area, should be a signal to refrain from having sex and an impetus to see a doctor immediately.

Since VD was a serious problem among Canadian troops, one general suggested the creation of a brothel brigade in which women would be regularly screened for sexual diseases. The idea was scrapped mostly because of possible negative reactions from the home front.

Raymond told Uncle Mike of his experience with fast girls, even though he knew of Uncle Mike's work with preventative measures. "I went down a road and here were some brothels doing a fine trade. And one of us blokes said, 'Is that one of them places? Why aren't we goin' in?'

"So, we went in and there was a garish sort of thing, a big wench with a short blue dress on, a miniskirt which I'd never seen a woman wear. Came and sat on my knee and said, 'Hey soldier, English soldier, you like nice girl?' After I bought her a drink, she said, 'You come upstairs with me.' And there was a big, central stairs and there was a long trek of soldiers goin' up and comin' down.

"And there was this girl who was just sort of playing with my hat, you know, and then patting my face and saying, 'You like nice French and Italian girl?' and so on. And I thought to myself, 'I wonder what it's like?' She said she wanted a limoncello. And I said to her, 'Limoncello, pas bonne pour la mademoiselle.' She said, 'No, but good for making love.'

"And as I was going further up the stairs with her, I saw this character from our lot who had VD. And I looked at that guy and I thought, 'Right, Raymond, you nearly went with this wench.'

"So, I said. 'Allez, fini.' I'll always remember that her charm quickly turned off as she parted with, 'You fuck off, you no fucking bon!' And so, I am still moral in my army life. A smart guy from our company had told me, 'A minute with Venus, a year with Mercury. Don't judge a package from its wrapping. Young, pretty, easy, but full of germs.'"

DRIVING TRUCK

Over time Uncle Mike was promoted, at least he thought so, given a job he preferred, driving truck. "I heard that General Motors and Ford Motors of Canada cooperated to make lots of military vehicles, with interchangeable parts. My army truck was an entirely Canadian design, had the two flat panes of the windshield angled slightly downward to minimize the glare from the sun and to avoid causing strong reflections that would be observable from aircraft."

The pug-nosed design was according to British specifications for a compact truck that would be more efficient to transport by ship. The specifications also demanded right-hand drive. Since the cab had to accommodate the comparatively large North American engines, it was cramped but Uncle Mike liked the job of trucking supplies.

He wrote home only in general terms about his truck driving in the armed forces. We wondered about the material covered with a black pen but approved eventually by a censor on the envelope. Even when he returned home after the war, he gave only brief hints about his work, mostly about his hatred of working on the anti-malaria and venereal disease details. He suppressed information about events of a more personal nature. But he waxed eloquent generally about his fascination with driving truck to provide supplies.

RAYMOND KILLED

At an informal wedding reception at his family farm for one of his friends, and after drinking quite a bit of alcohol, Uncle Mike's tongue was loosened. He recalled the cows and birds that bombs killed. Animals died of hunger and thirst on transport ships after standing in their own waste. Oil spills killed many fish and sea birds. Animals were used as mine sniffers or carriers of bombs.

But even under the influence of alcohol, Mike was reluctant to give details of his most nerve-wracking experience. The day had begun quietly, he recounted. He was telling Raymond of his expedition to spray water holes for malaria. Raymond recounted the bodies he had passed on his days on the front. Many were not identified because they were not identifiable.

"You know the mess that a direct hit by a shell does to a guy," Raymond recalled. "I have seen the effects of a mine, or a solid hit with a grenade. All that is left is a leg or a hunk of an arm. Some were thrown high in the air."

Raymond's stories became more gruesome as he told of soldiers lying on the field for weeks at a time. "Their blood started to rot and when you moved the bodies, stinking blood oozed out of their noses and mouths. By the time we got to other dead comrades, they had started to bloat in the sun and became so big that they bust their buttons. Their skin got blue and started to peel.

"What a stench. You never get used to it. The stink gets into your clothes and you can taste it in your mouth. If our politicians and generals smelled that we would not have any more wars."

And then Uncle Mike came to the part he had avoided for several years. He gave the gory details surrounding the death of his friend, Raymond, who was blown apart while standing next to him. All that remained were remnants of his limbs for the explosives reduced him to chunks of flesh and bone. "I could not believe it. Once he was alive and talking to me and then he was cut to bits and gone. I never got over that experience and never told anyone until now.

"I could accept the deaths of many of my fellows, but Raymond's was different. We had shared so many intimate moments and now I realized what his death would mean to his parents and to his brothers and sisters. Their lives would be changed forever.

"After hearing Raymond's stories and seeing terrible things myself, I began to have second thoughts about my involvement in the war and war in general," Uncle Mike concluded. "I could sympathize with those who willingly exposed themselves to malaria so they would be removed from battle, with those who pretended that they were sick, with those whose nerves could not take the war any longer. Soldiers had confessed to me that they were so frightened they peed and crapped their pants. They did not want to lie beneath the earth, but to walk on it, and not with crutches either.

"I heard about different treatments including electric shock, but also hospitals involving rest, fresh air, warm baths, good food and diversion. Soldiers recuperating could do some gardening, plant vegetables, raise chickens, play tennis, do woodworking or metal work.

"I began to understand that every man, no matter his background, his education, his class, had a breaking point. They could reach a last straw on an utterly exhausted nervous system. I understood why some soldiers felt they had to get out of this mess, why some pretended to be sick so they could be hospitalized some distance away, why others deserted for they could not take it any longer, why some hoped they would be diagnosed as crazy, for a mental hospital even though it was like a prison would be better than this.

"I thought of the politicians and generals who were directing the war effort. They made sacrifices to be sure, but they did not experience what Raymond and I experienced, this sickening reality. They had ideas, principles and plans which they pursued in great safety.

"I remember when Raymond and I marched joyfully to military music. From my time on the farm, to my training and movement to the front, I was a romantic about war. It was a great way to see the world, to do important deeds for my country, to gain honor and prestige. I felt that the whole country was behind me to rout the Nazis. I went to war for Canada's glory, but I experienced it instead as gory. I was young and had a lot of energy, but I was naive. In war some people get hurt; it is terrible.

"During fighting the Hitler war, I felt I had forgotten the values of love and caring in our home, in our church and in our community. On the farm, killing was reserved for animals and not for humans. But here, we were out to kill, to do violence to the enemy who were innocent pawns as we were. We were killing so many civilians and making many women widows, and children orphans. I began to hear the shrieks of the wounded as they writhed in pain. True, my malaria mission and VD detail were geared to help fellow soldiers, but it was all in the context of war.

"I never thought that we and the enemy had so much fire power. I now know that we were producing lots of deadly weapons which would lead to the production of human corpses and the leveling of buildings. What a chaos! What kind of meaning can emerge from such destruction?

"I had hoped that I would grow up as a young man, but I now felt that the war was paralyzing my courage and deadening my spirit. Even though my personal guilt was somewhat dimmed because what I was doing was for my country, I could not escape the sense of personal responsibility for what I was doing.

"Raymond had told me of the times he heard a smothered moan, a faint cry for help. Some of the wounded were begging for a smoke, a cup of water; some cried to God for pity. Some asked for a friendly hand to finish what the enemy had begun. Some were delirious, murmuring the names of loved ones. Many times, Raymond could do little more than prop a head on the body of another or pull the flap of his coat over a face to ward off a chilling wind.

"In the trenches, things were obviously freaky. How does one take a crap? I tried a corner of the trench; I tried it on a piece of paper, in my army bag. For reasons of nicety and politeness and avoiding embarrassment, a fellow soldier went above the trench to do his job; he was killed while crepitating, in a crouching position! It was a cruel trick of fate for he seemed the happiest one, the one with a promising future.

"I pondered on this horror, now so numerous, for blood-soaked earth has a glaring truth about it. Many soldiers were gone like Raymond and perhaps almost forgotten. I felt grateful that I was not hit; however, I was anything but unscathed. Why should I be spared and have the luxury of life? Peace and ease should be his reward, not mine. I could not talk about it. If I survived, even with wounds, or because of them, I would merit the admiration of my country. But, in some way my suffering was increased by a lack of bodily wounds. My mind was becoming shattered by war.

"A fellow Canadian who had a feel for poetry reminded me of Robert Graves who had been a combatant and had a choice name for the front: "the sausage machine." His reason for such a comparison: because it was fed with live men, churned out corpses, and remained firmly screwed in place.

BACK IN CANADA

"I was given an honorable discharge. My military character was regarded as excellent. I qualified for these campaign stars and medals: 1939–45 Star, the Italy Star, the Canadian Volunteer Service Medal and Clasp, the British War Medal, and the Defence Medal.

"But Private Mike was now Mr. Mike. I got a heroes' reception as we hit the shores of Canada. At the discharge depot, I learned that The Veterans' Land Act provided low-cost loans to veterans who wanted to purchase farm land, machinery, livestock and building materials in order to re-establish us after the war. I had my eye on mixed farming, that is, grain and cattle.

"And then it was so good to be back on the farm, for there is no place like home. My parents and siblings were so eager to welcome me back. I had some money and quickly purchased a new Ford truck and I had some ambition and trust in myself as I began to plan to build a retirement home for my parents in our neighbouring hamlet."

5

Social life

SHELTERED AND SIMPLE TOUGH TIMES

FARM LIFE WAS SIMPLE, providing a sheltered and often romantic atmosphere. Going to town in the winter was one of those lazy, idyllic times when Louie and David shopped, bought a bag of unshelled peanuts, tied up the lines and let the horses trot or walk at their own pace; they shelled and munched contentedly.

A cozy time was making the 10-mile trek to church for midnight Mass. Getting the electric lamp from one of the hibernating tractors, perching it on top of the caboose, connecting it to a six-volt battery, making a fire in the stove, driving in the moon-lit night with horses snorting steam into the enveloping dark, unhitching the horses and running them to the cold barns at the bottom of the hill, listening to the hiss of gas lamps and to new strains from the choir, Father Bernard clunking around the altar with his overshoe buckles clicking, Frank answering the German prayers lower and louder than the rest.

A memorable time was the bustle of threshing time, the camaraderie of muscled friends and neighbours, the freshly baked bread, the grain, fruit of one's labor, slipping between one's fingers. David caught the fever of harvest, especially, when in 1949 his Dad slipped off a ladder while painting the combine shed and broke vertebrae in his back. Although only 11, he got a taste of driving the self-propelled combine, and especially the car of the new manager of the farm, Uncle Frank. Louie, ever mechanically skillful, was always available for advice, even from his hospital bed.

There were many touching times. Neighbour Barney had all kinds of images about prairie life. "Sometimes I was so hungry I could eat a coyote and think it was a chicken. Ordinarily, since the soil is so rich, I could plant and harvest buttons. I hoped for a bumper crop, but this spring the ground had only a little moisture from the melted snow but no rain after it sprouted. Well, the seeds grew a little and we got 79 stooks in total. Lo and behold, it then rained for the next month and the second growth was higher than the stooks. It was good for hay.

"So, farming has its ups, mostly downs, except for the wind. Pioneer farmers are like flies caught in flypaper. Me, the second generation, are a lost generation. But tough times make us hang together, and we didn't starve but kept the wolf from the door.

"Those damn politicians and business outfits in eastern Canada. They make sure they make a profit over everything. Take our wheat. We have to pay to ship it East and then they make us pay for shipping milled products West, and at a high price. How come we have to pay them to ship cars and tractors to the West? These big and high muck-mucks make sure they never come out of the short end of the stick. They never lose their shirts. I try to be honest, for I have no axe to grind."

AN UNDERSTANDING TOOTH FAIRY

At five years, time for many eventful things. One in particular stands out for David: losing his first tooth. He considered it as an anticipated event, imagined, much discussed during the past month as he wiggled the tooth. It was the second day of school, and an auspicious timing. One bite on a peanut butter and jam sandwich and presto, outo. Also momentous was the fact that he was the first in his class to lose one.

As David drove home in his cart, he proudly felt the envelope in his pocket which contained the important relic. He was shaking with excitement as he stopped the cart in the yard and without unhitching his horse ran to display it to his mother. During supper, he repeatedly felt his pocket to make sure his treasure was still there. As he went to bed that evening, he anticipated slowly extricating it from his pocket and from the envelope. He wanted to place it carefully under his pillow, but it was gone.

"Mom, I can't find my tooth," he shouted downstairs. "I placed it in a dip in the blanket and now it is gone," he said between sobs.

Together Anne and David moved the mat in front of the bed, gingerly lifted the blanket, searched the mattress. No tooth! Now it seemed as if the tooth fairy's long-awaited visit would not happen.

"Oh, the tooth fairy will know that the tooth fell out and is now lost," Mom assured him.

He eventually became convinced that the best course of action was to go to sleep to hasten the arrival of the tooth fairy. But he continued to toss and turn, and periodically assured his mother, "I'm sleeping now!"

Anne was moved by his predicament. She was at best only a half-believer in the fairy, but a sufficient one to pencil a letter of explanation to the fairy, requesting that she leave the money for him because he deserved it even though there was no evidence that it had fallen out. If David was in doubt about the visitation of the fairy, she could at least assure him that she had tried.

"Dear Tooth Fairy," she penned.

"Please, my son lost his tooth, and please still give him money because it is so important to him. Please, please.

"If you are a good and kind fairy, you should give it to him without question. Think about it. Sincerely, Anne.

"In my playful mood, I thought at first I should threaten the fairy to give David the money or else. But we have to give him some money regardless," she thought. This complication both puzzled and delighted Louie.

Anne checked on David and found that he was still not sleeping. She comforted him and told him about the letter assuring him that the tooth fairy would understand.

In the morning, David found not one but two coins under his pillow. He was thrilled with the fairy's generosity and gently rubbed the coins together. He hurried to put them in his piggy bank.

VISITING THE GRANDPARENTS

David and Theresa were born near the households of their grandparents. During several seasons, there was little rain and farmers sometimes could not produce enough seed to sow for the next crop. Louie was creative and he searched for other employment opportunities. He went to Chicago to take a vocational training course and received a certificate in Diesel Auto and Engines program.

Then he went by train to Toronto, found that jobs were scarce and so he returned to the farm. Later, both Anne and Louie went to Toronto and succeeded in finding employment. They returned with presents: a girl's tricycle for Theresa and a boy's for David.

While the parents went to work in Toronto, Theresa and David stayed at their grandparents' farm. David was quite a handful. He watched with fascination as Grandpa lit his pipe with a kindling stick which he kept on the cook stove. It was an economical measure designed to save on matches.

On another occasion, Grandma used a real match to light the evening lamp. David wanted to have one to do the same. She showed him, using the wrong end of the match, that the match would not light. David knew it was a trick, but what could he do? Cry or throw a tantrum?

Later, when the family settled on the farm, they visited their grandparents, retired now in two different villages. These were joyous occasions. Grandma always gave grandchildren candy. One winter day the family made the 38-mile (the neighbour loaned them his car on another occasion) round trip by horses and caboose to Anne's parents. In the village, Louie had to make a detour through some unchartered snow and the caboose hit a solid steel post. David was catapulted into the window, suffered a large cut on his forehead and was treated in the drugstore by the local nurse. He cried but as consolation he could pick out a chocolate bar.

As children, David and Theresa did not visit their neighbours very often and did not play with their children. Anne thought they might make nuisances of themselves there. Instead, the family regularly visited their relatives, one time, Anne's side and the other, Louie's. The family tried to get away early on Sunday afternoon, shortly after Louie's nap, in order to beat their relatives' visits. Sometimes those relatives would check the farm, find no one at home, and then come to the same place that they were visiting.

ROLLING SMOKES

Smoking cigarettes was commonplace among prairie men, among boys, a little. Among women, not so much, and among girls, not at all. Tailor-made cigarettes were rather rare mostly because of their expense. Many farmers rolled their own cigarettes by hand. This process gave control over the size of the cigarette. Cigarette smoking was a ritual and commenting on the weather, sharing gossip and the state of the crops went conveniently with its performance.

There was relaxation and contentment in the smoking process especially during an evening after supper. Louie purchased processed loose-leaf tobacco in a tin can along with a single pack or a carton of rolling paper. He unscrewed the lid, opened its encasing, lifted fingerfuls of tobacco and inserted them into a pouch, or put the tobacco directly into a rolling paper.

Louie sometimes gave advice about rolling smokes. "Don't be in a hurry for you will scatter some of that precious ingredient. Hold the rolling paper with the glued edge away from you. Rest one end of the rolling paper between your thumb and middle finger," he demonstrated.

"Hold the paper in the crease with your index finger of the same hand. Use the other hand to adjust the paper into the open chute, then insert judicious amounts of tobacco into this leaf, spreading it and rolling the paper to ensure it is evenly spread. This requires some skill and practice.

"Work from one end to the other. Hold it steady so you don't spill any tobacco. If needed, even out the tobacco along the paper to make it consistent. Getting it as level as possible helps the cigarette burn more smoothly. If it is damp or clumped, gently pick apart any lumps with your fingers.

"My index finger in the crease stabilizes the paper as I add tobacco, and it will also keep tobacco from spilling out the ends. One end will become the tip of the cigarette, the part that you light. Pack the tobacco as you want. Begin to roll the cigarette between the thumb and middle finger. Shape it, compress the tobacco and roll the paper tightly. The front edge of the paper should tuck snugly behind the tobacco as you begin to roll. This may take a few tries. Just keep moving the front of the paper up and down, and gently push in with the thumbs until it catches.

"Roll the cigarette until only the adhesive end of the paper remains. Activate the adhesive by licking all the way along its edge; think of it like sealing an envelope. When the adhesive is wet, roll the rest of the paper until no edge remains. Seal the cigarette by applying even pressure: run your fingers along the length of the cigarette, and gently but firmly press the adhesive until it sticks. Make sure not to bend, tear, or crinkle the paper. Twisting the tip that you light will prevent the tobacco from falling out of a poorly-packed cigarette. Twisting the tip from which you smoke will keep tobacco from sticking to your lips."

Some farmers were content with using only a meager amount of tobacco in their cigarettes, but Louie wanted a thick, fat one. A thicker one was harder to seal and harder to draw the smoke through the cigarette.

Farmers rolled a cigarette whenever they wanted to smoke, or they pre-rolled a bunch so that they didn't need to do the work each time. Some smokers found the act of hand-rolling a useful way to limit their cigarette consumption; it is harder to chain-smoke if they had to spend several minutes rolling each cigarette.

"Now you can light your cigarette," Louie continued. "Get a match from your pocket, draw your fingernail over its white end or rub it on a hard surface or on your pants. Away you go, now you can puff. The aroma of tobacco is intoxicating."

Louie used this ritual many times and always had loose matches in his pocket. As he was carrying a five-gallon can of cream to the railway station one evening, he held and moved the can close to his pocket and the matches ignited. He felt the heat, saw the smoke and swatted the area with repeated hard blows; this extinguished the fire but not before he burned parts of his hands. In the future, he carried matches in a small box to prevent such an accident.

GRANDMA'S DEATH

Rural life can be lonely, and when people are far from friends, isolated from neighbours, tragedy seems so much more intense. Death can occur from accident or disease, from a deliberate act of frustration or it could be from nature on the rampage. When death occurred, prairie people converged to help. The police came to give authority to the scene, and when it was over, the damage repaired, the crisis resolved, the brown earth smoothed over the grave, life went on.

Rural people heard of a neighbour who froze in the snow. With storms, it was easy to become snow blind. Or, someone lives alone, the fire goes out, he is too weak to stoke it. The neighbour does not see smoke coming from the chimney for a couple of days. "If cold doesn't get the poor buggers, then they suffocate to death from coal oil fumes," neighbour Barney noted. "The wife said I give them a little money when I see them."

As David remembered her, Grandma was always overweight. She liked to drink a lot of water from the common pail with the common dipper. She informed David that she gained weight because of all the water she drank;

he knew otherwise. She became increasingly immobile, required Istvan to help her put on her stockings in the morning, sat in her chair to peel the potatoes, and asked her sons to get her pills. She became delirious, unable to do her regular household chores and was confined to her bed.

Everyone knew she was dying and were vocal in her presence, saying the rosary, and discussing how they should word her obituary. They thought they knew her full name, that is, her first name and original surname. As her son, Frank, was writing it down, she regained consciousness, opened her eyes wide and shouted, "It is Vass; I want Vass in there." With that she closed her eyes and died. But the full name was included in the final obituary for she had the last word about her own life and death.

GOOD OLD EATON'S CATALOGUE

The Eaton's catalogue was an important item in the household, as a dictionary, a reference for purchases, as a doorstop, as reading material in the outside toilet. In one of his prairie paintings, William Kurelek sketches the Eaton's catalogue hanging on the wall of such a toilet. Indeed, old catalogues were also used instead of toilet paper before bathrooms were common in homes. While sitting on a hole, they could also thumb its pages for interesting items.

No wonder it was called the homesteader's bible, for rural residents could use it to order goods that had previously been available only in larger Canadian cities. To order these goods one had to follow the mail order sheet: give the catalogue article number, its quantity, colour, size (do not forget), name of article, page, price of each, and the nearest railway station. Orders were forwarded to Winnipeg, filled promptly, sent, and received COD, cash on delivery, all in a few days.

Its founder, Timothy Eaton's philosophy was the greatest good for the greatest number of people. He proclaimed satisfaction or money refunded. The whole West was his customer. One could purchase almost anything a farmer needed: kerosene, paraffin, raisins, dried prunes, biscuits, but it could not provide the smell!

The various yearly catalogues featured a wealth of photographs showing eye-catching, groovy fashions, the styles of the times. Its portrayal and its descriptions tried to entice buyers with words such as: We used a superbly soft and lovely rayon alpaca weave, with striped rayon for the brilliant contrast. A short sleeve dress is beautifully detailed with exquisite tucking in the bodice and pockets, and graceful pleats in the skirt. If prairie women could not afford these smart dresses, they could use them as patterns to sew their own, although sometimes the catalogue one was ordered first.

Initially at least, Eaton's mirrored details of rural life. No bathtubs but a dib and dab out of a bucket on Saturday night before going to town. No underarm deodorant. While its main stores did not give the smells of dung-laden boots, it emanated, nevertheless, its unique friendly but metaphorical smell and the farmers felt it was the right one, reminding them of home.

The catalogue displayed plan books for ideal homes and barns in the West. The best building material at wholesale prices could be shipped directly from British Columbia. Again, these plans could furnish ideas for moving from log structures to a fitting frame home.

As noted earlier, its page provided uses additional to an ordering manual: as readers in many classrooms, as shin pads fixed with canning rings for playing hockey, as images to use as paper dolls or as crafting items for school projects. Newcomers to Canada could use it to gain facility with the English language. There were other practical purposes: to help insulate drafty cabins and houses, and, for viewing, the lingerie and swimsuit sections.

While the catalogue was depicted in Kurelek's painting, and was mailed into the hearts and the memory of rural Canadians, it made its way into its literature also. In Lucy Maud Montgomery's novel, *Anne's House of Dreams*, there is disagreement over how morally tolerable some images in the catalogue are. In Roch Carrier's story, The Hockey Sweater, a mother mistakenly receives from Eaton's a despised Toronto Maple Leaf's sweater for her Montreal Canadiens' son.

On the cover of an alluring, coloured cover of the Eaton's Christmas Wishbook Catalogue is a mother sitting on a large armchair in a red flowing gown; she is helping her son in house coat open a Christmas present while father and older sister in quasi-formal attire watch attentively. In the background is a Christmas tree decorated with ample streamers and large silver bulbs.

The Eaton's catalogues were indeed indispensable for a prairie household.

DRIVING TO BEAT 60

For David a lot of farm life centred on cars. He remembers driving to school with a horse and cart and encountering a Model T proudly driven by an old, dark and tall gentleman with his prim, hatted lady friend sitting contentedly beside him. It had a putt putt, purring sound as it sped by. Memorable was a ride a former pupil gave him in his family's Model A, an improvement on the T but one which required a rather skillful touch to shift gears. He often tried but seldom succeeded to beat 60.

While on his parents' homestead, Louie went to an auction sale in town. He took along his savings, $52. He succeeded in buying for $50 a Model T that needed repair. He took pride in restoring it and now the farm had two of them. Brother Peter, not adept at things mechanical, wrecked his family vehicle and Grandpa persuaded Louie to give his T for the family's use. He did so, on condition that Peter never be permitted to drive it.

When farming on his own, Louie purchased a practical International speed wagon truck that, while not having a large box, had a high gear ratio. It was like a convertible with celluloid side windows and a canvas top. It had a secure holder for David to hang on to when he was invited to travel along.

Another vehicle: again, Louie was in a practical vein, for instead of purchasing a car he went for a rather large and new Studebaker truck. The company billed it as soundly built and exceptionally good looking, rugged, powerful and thrifty. It had manufactured 200,000 military vehicles for use on some of the toughest assignments during the war.

It was a smashing black and red but needed a box which Louie built and painted in complementary colours. He put brackets atop the box and affixed a loader to be driven by the motor's power takeoff. Instead of a mere 25 bushels with the speed wagon, he could now haul over 100 bushels, loaded not by hand but by this augur. Neighbours hired him to haul their grain to the elevator. These vehicles were followed by the purchase of a new Ford Meteor car with its classy chrome grill and bumpers, sun visor, wide body, overdrive, radio and clock. Succeeded by a Ford Customline with automatic transmission.

MANY ANIMALS

David and Theresa took animals for granted. There was a great variety of them on their farm. Unlike their parents, Louie and Anne did not eat rabbits, but they kept them in cages and they provided nourishment for their chickens. Other animals, while endearing but preeminently nurtured for their food value were turkeys, chickens, ducks, pigs, cows.

The spring chicks were a welcome sight for the Louie-Anne children. The family had only one dog at a time for Louie valued it primarily for its utility. With more than one, he reasoned, there would be a lot of frivolity and little concentration on the tasks at hand.

BUSY AT KNITTING

From her mother, Anne learned to find needed tasks, apply her hands and mind to them and keep busy. She often said she was hooked by the lure of crocheting, and then she laughed; she embroidered edgings on pillow slips and crotched beautiful decorative doilies from elaborate pineapple designs. She was a highly productive crafter, knitting socks, afghans, shawls, scarves, mittens and bedspreads.

"When my hands are busy, my mind stays focused on the here and now. It gives me time to solve problems and helps me calm down," she stated. The repetitive actions of needlework induced a relaxed state like that of meditation and yoga. These creative actions lowered her heart rate and blood pressure. The results were useful products which enhanced self-esteem.

"I like to think it helps control my weight, keep my fingers flexible. I also like being able to discuss clothing and doilie patterns with my sisters and compare the results." Flour bags provided material for everyday dresses, bed sheets and tea towels.

"In order to change and adapt my clothes, I did some make-over dresses. Younger folks painted their legs to look like expensive stockings."

She procured wool from her parents' homestead farm, picked out the straw and burs, washed it and got David to help card it and, then while everyone was sound asleep, she sat at the spinning wheel and spun the raw wool into yarn. She was adept at making soap, first cooking tallow, then adding lye water, eventually pouring it into large containers, heating it, and cutting it when hard. It was excellent for washing clothes.

She used down and feathers from geese and ducks, called dunya feather ticking, to fill pillows and covers. "I hardly have any time to have a game of cards," she concluded.

JESUS KNEW HOW TO COOK

David remembers one of Father Bernard's sermons. Its theme followed part of the Our Father asking for daily bread. According to this pastor, Jesus took his Father's advice seriously and ensured that his friends had good meals. So, while he learned carpentry skills from his father, he also prized the recipes and advice his mother gave him. On his mission he and the women following him cooked for the disciples for he was the good shepherd who cared for them and provided them with nourishing food.

Jesus' many stories indicate that he knew the secrets and traditions of the culinary art. For example, he knew the precise dose of yeast to be added to flour in making bread. He understood the nutritional properties of bread and fish, multiplied them for his guests and exalted the pleasure of eating them. And this multiplication account is important for it appears six times in the Scriptures.

As a good guest at the wedding feast of Cana, he ensured that the bridal party not be embarrassed for he provided tasty and abundant wine when the supply ran short. He was the waiter and washed his disciples' feet and shared himself by breaking bread at the last supper. After the resurrection, he stoked a charcoal fire to prepare fish for his disciples. Come have breakfast, he seemed to say. He told everyone that feasts are a foretaste of the heavenly future.

RE-LEARNING HUNGARIAN

Hungarian was David's first language. It was the main language used in his grandparents' home when he and his sister, Theresa, stayed with them for six months. Later, they stopped using it when they prepared to enter grade school. Their parents, Louie and Anne, no longer communicated in Hungarian with their children but only between themselves and with their relatives.

Once a year the Anne-Louie family visited Louie' aunt, Mary, in a neighbouring town. She and her husband Michael were welcoming relatives. Mary's cooking was out of this world and she eagerly showed anyone interested or not her fast-growing and productive garden. To ensure quick and abundant growth she nursed plants by physically touching them tenderly and moving the surrounding soil periodically.

Uncle Michael led Louie and David to his blacksmith shop right across the street. It was clean and orderly and he showed his craftsmanship, for in the old country he had learned several trades including blacksmithing, tinsmithing and mechanics. In a corner was a reconditioned Model T motor and parked in the back of the shop, his polished 1938 Dodge half-ton truck.

During the conversation in their home, Mary learned that David and Theresa no longer spoke Hungarian. She was appalled and quickly responded to this lack when she learned that David showed some inclination to relearn his Hungarian. To that end, she went to her bookcase and plied him with books to remedy the situation. Uppermost was the necessity to regain remedial religious knowledge in Hungarian. So, she gave him a little catechism, *Római Katholikus Kis Katekizmus,* and a prayerbook printed in Cleveland, *Imakönyv, Paduai Szent Antal.*

But Mary was not finished. She brought out her own bible, both Old and New Testaments, *Szent Biblia.* Then, a reader for North American Hungarians, inscribed with her husband's writing, *Amerikai Magyar fiú Magyarorsagon.* As if Mary had prepared for this event, she handed David a book that presupposed he as a Hungarian was about to learn English in 90 days: *Tanuljunk, Könnyen, Gyorsan, Angoglul!*

"Let me help you remember a few Hungarian words," she offered: Sweet dreams: *édes álmok,* and good night, *jó éjszakát."*

While David and Theresa remembered the good night greeting, they were both overwhelmed and grateful for this solicitude and magnanimity. Their parents were less than enthusiastic in reteaching them their native language and continuing to speak it. They had deliberately taught them English before they went to grade school and ceased speaking to them in Hungarian some time ago. After all, they were now in Canada and not in Hungary.

Later, while visiting a Hungarian community gathering, David heard there was a doctor in the group who was born in Hungary. He thought he could try a few words of his trial language and get a conversation going. He approached him gingerly, saying Good Day and How are you? The doctor looked at him in dismay and did not engage in any pleasantries. Instead, he said, "I don't speak Hungarian any more for it is the most useless language in the world." Not much encouragement for David here.

At home, David continued with the aunt's enthusiasm, using especially the Hungarian-English learning book. He tried to couple his learning with attempts to speak rather unsuccessfully with his parents and listening to Hungarian broadcasts on shortwave radio. But enthusiasm went only so far and the learning petered out after a few months and there were no more visits to his great aunt.

MOVIE IMITATING HITLER

During school, David got word that there would be a movie in the town hall on Saturday evening. Louie and Anne thought he could attend and so dropped him off while they did the shopping. As he was waiting for the hall to open and was talking with his cousins who were in line, one of the local boys, nicknamed Baldie because of his short hair, started pushing David around. David was used to jostling in fun, but this appeared to be serious. What to do? He let Baldie tussle with him but soon realized that Baldie was both a town boy and shorter than he was. In his estimation, farm boys had more muscles than their town counterparts. So, he pulled Baldie down and sat on him. A victory of sorts.

The screen for the movie was four white sheets sewn together and attached to a two-by-four frame. David hoped this talkie would be an improvement on the silent ones he had seen before. The movie was The Great Dictator by Charlie Chaplin. In it, the actor stars in a dual role as a nameless, humble and forgetful Jewish barber and also as an autocrat, Adenoid Hynkel, dictator of Tomania, with a flag resembling the swastika.

Norman, a town resident, also in the movie line, had seen this one before and had read about comedian Chaplin and this, his first talkie movie. "Chaplin imitates Adolph Hitler," Norman interjected. "He bears a striking resemblance to him especially with his shnu bart moustache. Chaplin was fascinated with his uncanny connections to the Fuehrer/Phooey, for Chaplin was born in the same week as Hitler in April 1889. Both fought for causes, one for good and the other for evil.

"Hitler's German ministers are Garbitsch and Herring, modeled after Joseph Goebbels and Hermann Goering, respectively," Norman added. "Benzino Napaloni, dictator of the neighbouring country of Bacteria, is a satirical portrayal of Italy's Benito Mussolini. I like the scene where Hynkel, as Hitler, dances with a balloon of the world to the music of Richard Wagner, revealing his fragile ego as the balloon bursts. Chaplin was hard not only on these two dictators but on every one who followed those goose steps.

"The film was banned in Germany in 1940 when it was made. But there was a chance it might also be banned in Great Britain and in the

United States. However, Chaplin's serious message became a smashing success. It is a visionary movie.

"In one scene, the Storm Troopers pelt washerwoman, Hannah (played by Chaplin's wife), with tomatoes which they have just stolen from a grocery store. It shows cowardly bullying at its best or worst. Chaplin moves so quickly between slapstick and chilling horror, but I shouldn't give away too much of the film," Norman concluded.

Everyone enjoyed it.

SKIMPY GIFTS FOR WEDDING

The Anne-Louie family was invited to the wedding of Anne's youngest brother. The reception was held at the original family homestead farm. There had been no wedding shower and the wedding gifts were rather skimpy for it was during the depression period. Farm families pledged what they could: live chickens to provide eggs for breakfast, or clucking hens that would furnish eggs for incubation; enamel ware, little pots, pans, a dipper, basin, kettle, towels or table cloths. A few gave more expensive gifts such as a china tea set. Parents gave a healthy cow and a team of horses.

FIRE AND BRIMSTONE SERMON

David's grandfather helped finance a new church building. The upper church featured carved oak benches. Males sat on the right side and females and children on the left. Uncle Frank, always a contrarian, sat conspicuously with the women.

The church's architectural plan was based on a pattern from California and, while a tall and dignified Gothic-like structure, it was ill-suited for winter weather. Come October and November, worship services moved into the basement, heated by three wood stoves made from oil drums. Here ceilings were low and the cement floor cold, so pastor Bernard decided to have another go with the upstairs. He installed a furnace for this area and hoped that would make it comfortable on Sundays. But, no, the cold was stronger than the forced warm air. So down to the basement again.

It was customary to have a parish mission just before harvest time. A missionary would give a talk followed by Benediction with the Blessed Sacrament. David remembers one fiery preacher. He had confidence in his forceful voice for the church did not have a public address system. He tried to give his fire and brimstone talk from the pulpit, but, alas, his words echoed back and forth.

He tried again to blast from the communion railing near the congregation. Again, his words reverberated. In frustration, he resorted to an unaccustomed whisper. It worked, or seemed to, for he was not sure he was communicating. One consolation that male members had was that after the sermon they could listen to a boxing match featuring Joe Louis on a radio and speakers on the church steps. Meanwhile the Christian Mothers met to prepare menus for the annual fowl supper.

A TREASURED BIKE

Hired hand Janos never drove a car or truck but instead rode a bicycle. It was shiny blue with a bell, kick stand, front carrier, and reflectors in front and back. David wanted to have such a bike and ride it; he pestered his parents about getting one. Early in his life he had a prized tricycle that his parents brought from Toronto, but now he was grown up and wanted to do grown up things and riding a bicycle was one of them.

The pestering worked. When Louie came home from a farm sale, he showed David his new purchase—a second-hand bike. It was a lady's bike, dull black in colour and did not have a bell, kick stand, a carrier or reflectors, but it was his. He took pride in owning it. Its handlebars were almost beyond his reach even when he stood on the pedals. Standing was possible since it had the curvature for women's skirts. The padded seat added to its height; in its stead, Louie put a lower flat board.

Now it was up to David's ingenuity to ride it. At first, he merely walked with it, feeling its frame and handle bars. It did have possibilities. He gave it a push, jumped on the pedals, but fell off with the bike tumbling upon him. A few bumps and bruises. After several days and many tries, he succeeded in pedaling a fair distance before falling again.

He had an idea: why not begin from the little hill in front of the house, push the bike, jump on it, keep his balance and begin pedaling. Yes, it was an exhilarating experience; he was moving down the hill, but he did not know how to stop. He closed his eyes as he ascended the steps in front of the house and fell over. Not too gracious, a few more bruises, but a first flight and the tires were still inflated. Many more attempts and falls, one ending in between the large wheel of the double box in the yard.

What a delight to be in control, at least somewhat, what fascination: self-propelled movement with the wind flowing through his hair! What freedom and independence! Although David ordinarily went to school with a cart and horse, he persuaded his parents that Theresa could manage this time while he went to school with his bike. Here he was with the older boys; during recess time he could ride with them around the school yard, but he still had some difficulty applying the brakes. As he scooted around a corner, he failed to stop and his bike hit a barbed wire fence and one of the barbs pierced the front tire. Alas, he could no longer ride it but had to push it home behind the cart. He did not disclose the cause of the flat tire and Louie quickly put a patch on the tube.

He went again to school on his bike. Whenever he could, he pedaled like crazy, flying unfettered through the air. Pedal power enabled him to see and be seen by the entire world, his whole life ahead of him. With adrenalin high, he traversed paths not entirely his own.

RECREATION/PICNICS

Since farm folk spent so much t time and energy to get all of the farm and housework done, they did not have a lot of time for entertainment. Despite or because of exhausting work, pioneer families, still found some joy in getting together. Such socializing included games, music and dancing, community picnics, going to church, and taking a trip to town.

Children often entertained themselves, but at school, especially during noon recess, they played games like follow the leader, blind man's bluff, and hide and seek. They played circle games like dodge ball, and ante ante over, hopscotch and jump rope. And, of course, softball, and foot hockey in winter.

If the weather kept them indoors, they played I spy, Simon says, or who's got the button, and foot hockey in the school basement. In the winter, children built snow forts or slid down snowbanks. When the yard was covered with freshly fallen snow, they enjoyed a game of fox and goose.

Occasions like weddings, dances, box socials, picnics, and school concerts brought people together. Neighbours organized work parties called bees to build houses, churches, or barns. Women organized bees for quilt making and sewing. On these communal occasions, after the work was completed, there was often a meal followed by singing or dancing.

Attending church services was one way that people were able to meet their neighbours, for the church helped to create a sense of community among the settlers. Before an actual church was built, people gathered at someone's home or at the school for services.

European immigrants brought their cultural musical instruments with them when they came to Canada. The violin or fiddle was one of the most popular instruments because it was small and lightweight. A fiddler supplied the music for many gatherings where people could enjoy singing and dancing. Other early instruments included the button accordion, guitar, banjo, mandolin, and also brass and woodwind instruments. The harmonica became popular because of its small size, low cost, and easy availability. It was perfect while travelling because it fit in a pocket.

When neighbours or relatives came for a visit, children played with each other and the men enjoyed a beer and their own gossip about farming while the women shared experiences of their children and prepared the main meal. Taking a trip to town was an opportunity to socialize with other adults.

There were only a few stores where pioneers could buy supplies, so families had to make or grow almost everything they needed. First, the pioneers had to break the prairie sod. Then they planted crops to feed the animals that fed the family.

Especially in winter when travelling was difficult, women, often felt very lonely. Symptoms of distress were crying, slovenly dress, and withdrawal from social interactions, with some instances of suicide. Cats and dogs provided some company, especially when a husband was away earning extra money. Children under foot were some everyday companionship and contentment.

The parish picnic was an important communal event. Besides being a gathering, it raised money for the church. It was the main fundraiser although the parish raised money in other ways; one was the Sunday collection; but it was almost negligible for many parishioners inserted only a nickel or so. Another was the annual church dues, an allotted amount for each individual or family. But the greatest was the annual parish picnic.

Parish picnics meant fun and food. Girls wore long white dresses with bows in their hair, some with the Toni formula, done up in the latest fashion depicted in magazines. A group of boys teased some of them, sometimes riled them, mean as snakes, and often tough as leather.

Although the picnics with their eating, drinking and fun appeared spontaneous and effortless, the parish group of Christian Mothers carefully planned and managed this grand affair. People from the surrounding district attended.

This event was even more grand in neighbouring parishes; there they included a band and a greased pig contest. In the latter, contestants tried to hold onto a slippery pig, sometimes in a mud pit. When they caught the pig, it became the prize itself. A kindred contest was climbing a greased pole. While these contests were entertaining, they did not raise much funds and they made dress clothes very slimy.

For her input into the event, Anne received (although addressed to Louie) a list of tasks and ingredients for the gathering. Among the extensive items were four chickens or six dollars, two pies and one cake, one loaf of sliced bread, jello fruit salad using three packages, two cans of corn, one can of pork and beans, a half-gallon of milk, a half-gallon of whipping cream, one kettle of peeled potatoes, one-half dozen boiled eggs, two quarts of fruit, garden lettuce or radish, two pounds of tomatoes, one bunch of celery, pickles, one bottle of ketchup. Cash could replace these items. In addition to preparing and supplying these items, Anne was given the task of serving the meat dishes, tomatoes and celery. Theresa was commissioned to set and work on table three and David was dubbed the coffee boy.

Under the brush-covered stands, the scrumptious meals with all the trimmings featured home-made ice cream, chicken or bratwurst, and beer.

The Saturday before the picnic or sometimes called a fowl supper, not to be confused with the odious kind, young men made outside preparations. They retrieved tables from storage, arranged the benches around them, cut leafy branches to protect the area from excessive sun rays and hoped it would not rain.

During the preparation of food, they watched a baseball game. Halfway through the game, everyone took a time out to grab a glass of beer and then resume the play.

After David had made his first round of serving coffee, he stood behind a group that was watching with fascination a game of chance featuring a mouse. On a table was a circular structure with little boxed enclosures and holes facing the inside. Tickets were sold corresponding to the little boxes and then a mouse released to find its way into a winning box. David wondered how the entertainer had managed to catch the puzzled mouse.

Then he noticed a couple emerging from the church bushes, joyful, playful but hoping to hide their tracks.

ADDITIONS TO FAMILY

Anne, Louie, Theresa and David welcomed additions to the family. David remembers one cold February morning when a neighbour came with news that Anne had given birth to a boy in the town hospital. The family welcomed that addition and the main task seemed to be to get sponsors for Gary and his baptism. Uncle Frank's snowmobile was in the yard and Louie made plans to visit would-be sponsors. The snowmobile's motor started quite easily and Louie and David jumped in.

It was David's first ride in this cold rig, not shielded from the penetrating cold weather. It skated along the well-trod horse tracks and arrived at another Uncle Frank and Aunt Margaret's home quite quickly. They were playing the card game smear with the neighbours and Louie joined in. Only after the neighbours departed did he announce the arrival of Gary and the request that Frank and Margaret be sponsors, which they readily agreed to. They had already heard that a birth was in the offing.

UNCLE FRANK'S AUCTION SALE

Louie and David went to an auction sale, a common social and commercial event in the rural area. But this was not just an ordinary auction sale. It was of a favorite uncle, the one who pitched into the farm operation when Louie broke his back.

While Uncle Frank followed meticulous instruction on how to carry out farm work, he was permissive in his ways with David. He was the one who instructed David on how to drive a car, steer the combine while he checked whether there was grain being thrown over and let David operate the tractor pulling the power binder. Later, he used his mechanical skills in a local implement dealership and now he had passed away.

Here David was at a sale of his belongings: two trucks, some tractors, a collection of guns, fishing rods, showy and tall bird houses and his trailer house and possessions. His whole life was laid out before buyers in rows of boxes. He had been in charge of Grandma and Grandpa's homestead. It had been a place of life, 11 boys and one girl. Here Uncle Frank made hootch at night among the trees. He was an example of honest, hard work, abstemious living, prudent management, and independence. These were the qualities that transformed the plains.

David felt emotional as Uncle Frank's possessions were up for auction, one by one, or several in boxes. Louie was not in need of any more possessions but he bought several fishing rods he remembered his brother using. As with most of the items, they were in great condition. Louie certainly wanted and got a framed photo of a recent family reunion, competing in bidding with other family members.

David had his eye on the elaborate and towering bird houses. They were not up for auction immediately and so he decided to visit his aunt in a nearby residence. When he returned to the auction, he found to his dismay that they had been sold.

Uncle Frank's tractors and truck sold for relatively high prices since as a mechanic he had carefully reconditioned them.

Conclusion

ENJOYING THE DARK

PRAIRIE LIFE WAS A reciprocity between light and dark. Farmers enjoyed the light. The first thing they erected after their farm was powered by electricity was a yard light. No longer did the family have to walk to the barn in the dark or with a kerosene lantern. The yard light was high enough to illumine the entrances to almost all the farm buildings and expose wild animals or unwanted humans.

David appreciated this illumination but remembered the good old days when there was no yard light, when even the moon had not yet appeared, when there was total darkness. Only the stars studded the night sky. In the winter, there was the glow of the snow but that did not interfere with the towering vault and the Orion constellation, an arm of a crowd of stars, the Milky Way galaxy.

In school, he had studied about that constellation and now he could count its stars. According to a Greek myth, Orion is a hunter and David could see his upraised sword, his shield and his belt. He had learned that these same stars were as much a part of his history as they were of cave men and wooly mammoths. Explorers travelled with the help of these stars, although humans benefitted from darkness; it was also a healthy reprieve from activities in the light and also helpful to wildlife and the environment. David treasured the rhythm of darkness and light, but total darkness, except for coal oil lamps, was welcome and a blessing!

There was a continuity between grandparents and their old country and present-day dwellers on the Prairies. This continuity consisted of trees both on the Hungarian puszta-village and also on the prairie landscape. There were native trees on the family farm. When Grandpa and Grandma began homesteading, they were happy that now they had enough wood to build a log house and lots for heating and cooking. But as they began to clear the land for sowing, they realized that trees were also a burden for they had to be chopped down, dragged away and their roots dug out, gathered and burned.

The most hated tree was the black poplar; it was generally large and tall and its tarry nature made it difficult to cut with an axe or saw. In spring, these trees unveiled snowy, downy flowers before their leaves sprouted. They proudly displayed these diamond-glowing triangular shapes, glossy green on both surfaces and notched at the ends. Black poplar trees grew rapidly in low-lying areas. Some had burrs on them, a deformed outgrowth on a trunk or branch. These abnormalities looked strange but could be considered beautiful and some artisans prized them.

Farmers valued poplar trees. They were easy to handle, relatively light in weight and soft. According to Louie, 200 years ago Carolus Lennaeus gave them the name poplar, according to the Latin word for people. He wrote that he chose the name because of their whispering, rustling leaves which reminded him of "the murmuring of a great people." Their simple moss-green leaves with rounded and toothed edges turn golden in the fall and their bark is cracked or ridged. They form groves and grow fast but are short-lived.

Wild birch trees grew in clumps on the farm. They have a satiny texture, thin bark, and leaves that turn yellow in the fall. Indigenous peoples treasured their bark because of its little weight, flexibility and ease for stripping off trees. They used this bark to build strong, waterproof and lightweight canoes, bowls, wigwams, and as medicine for healing wounds by putting it directly on the skin. Grandpa liked it as firewood since it ignited readily and burned well; he also used it to smoke foods.

Willows were abundant on farm land especially near gravel pits. They form dense thickets near water and their pussy bombs appear before their long, narrow and spear-like leaves. Chewing on young twigs and bark can ease headache pain, heartburn and stomach ailments. Grandpa used one of its branches to form an arm for a towel rack and its branches for a broom. Their fuzzy buds make an attractive flower array indicating the early arrival of spring.

The family farm did not have a grove to protect them from the noise and dust of the main road and so they ordered and planted trees from the Indian Head nursery. As they grew, the caragana and poplar looked lush and attractive, formed a shelterbelt and windbreak, and assured privacy; they welcomed the birds that nested in them.

Various wild bushes furnished fruit: june berries (saskatoons) gave abundant, juicy and appetizing morsels and then some. The family knew that Native people used them to make pemmican; the family used them in a variety of ways—in pies, breads, jams and jellies. David picked a pailful, cleaned them and kept them for the fall; Anne used them in a cake to be presented to the teacher.

Less abundant were gooseberries which Theresa and David ate in the bushes. High bush cranberries, raspberries and small strawberries had an exceptional taste. Choke cherries and pin cherries unfolded their showy flowers and leaves but were sour tasting. All of these fruits displayed a diverse beauty supporting birds and butterflies.

While this family did not grow apples trees, their grandparents relished crabapples and small pears, cherries, plums and grapes.

Sometimes heavy, wet snow fell. Both the remaining leaves and the branches bore the slush and its overpowering weight and often came crashing to the ground. But the large and soggy flakes kept falling. There was no wind and the air was quiet. Some considered snow as messy, but David enjoyed running through it and getting his boots and pants wet. Fortunately, the temperature was warm and he did not freeze.

www.ingramcontent.com/pod-product-compliance
Lightning Source LLC
Chambersburg PA
CBHW071227260626
47162CB00004B/1455